WINTER IN BELLAPALMA

WINTER IN BELLAPALMA

*From the posthumous papers
of the writer Hans Berlow*

JENS BJØRNEBOE

*Translated from the Norwegian by
Esther Greenleaf Mürer*

Frayed Edge Press
Philadelphia, PA

Original title: *Vinter i Bellapalma*

First published in 1958 by Cappelens forlag, Oslo
Reprinted 1975 by PAX Forlag A/S, Oslo
©1975 by Jens Bjørneboe

English translation ©Esther Greenleaf Mürer
Published with the kind permission of Therese Bjørneboe

Cover illustration by Juliette van der Molen
Cover design by A.R. Melnik

This book is printed on acid-free paper

Publishers Cataloging-in-Publication

Names: Bjørneboe, Jens, 1920-1976. Vinter i Bellapalma. | Mürer, Esther Greenleaf, translator.
Title: Winter in Bellapalma / Jens Bjørneboe ; translated from the Norwegian by Esther Greenleaf Mürer.
Description: Philadelphia, PA : Frayed Edge Press, 2021. | Summary: Follows the exploits of a community of expatriates living off-season in a small Italian fishing village: their lives, loves, and interactions with the locals, including involvement in a dispute between the fishermen and the town fathers who wish to promote the tourist industry.
Identifiers: LCCN 2020946642 | ISBN 9781642510270 (pbk.) | ISBN 9781642510287 (ebook)
Subjects: LCSH: Expatriation--Fiction. | Friendship--Fiction. | Man-woman relationships--Fiction. | Travelers--Fiction. | Italy--Fiction. | BISAC: FICTION / Literary. | FICTION / Absurdist. | FICTION / Small Town & Rural.
Classification: LCC PT8950.B528 V56 2021| DDC 839.823 B557W--dc23
LC record available at https://lccn.loc.gov/ 2020946642

CONTENTS

Introduction

Jens Bjørneboe's *Winter in Bellapalma*: Hemingway Tribute and Harbinger of Works to Come

Esther Greenleaf Mürer

When a multi-pronged crisis plunged Norwegian author Jens Bjørneboe into a severe depression in 1957 it was to Italy he fled, remaining there for a year and a half. The comic novel *Winter in Bellapalma*, published in 1958, dates from this period. It is a tongue-in-cheek tribute to Hemingway (Bjørneboe had published the essay "Hemingway and the Beasts" three years earlier), and is uncharacteristically lighthearted for Bjørneboe. So different was it from the novels of social criticism for which he had become known that it was all but ignored in Norway at the time, and still tends to get short shrift in discussions of his work. And yet it prefigures his later writings in important ways.

Italy and Germany are the two cultures which most strongly impart a cosmopolitan flavor to Bjørneboe's writing; both crop up in his poetry, novels, essays, and plays. For Bjørneboe they have a polarity which finds its strongest expression in his two pivotal works from 1966, *Moment of Freedom* and *The Bird Lovers*.

Bjørneboe's knowledge and love of German culture was deep, but—because learning about Nazi atrocities at a vulnerable age had shocked him into his first awareness of human evil—intensely ambivalent. On the other hand, Italy stood for healing, in myriad ways which are detailed in his most complex work, Moment of Freedom. Leif Longum comments that, while Italy and its culture likewise play an important part in Bjørneboe's writings,

> this relationship is a happy one, free of the ambivalence he felt towards everything German. He hardly ever mentions Fascism, for instance, a surprising fact in view of his preoccupation with German Nazism and all it stands for. It is as if Fascism was just an unfortunate accident, unrelated to its Italian background.[1]

Among Bjørneboe's first published writings were a series of travel essays written in 1950 for the Oslo newspaper, *Aftenposten*. These often included drawings by the author, such as "A Trattoria in Florence." Since Bjørneboe at that time had recently made the transition from painting to writing, it is no surprise that Italy and its art loom large in his early poetry, with poems on Cimabue, Donatello, Michelangelo, Lorenzo the Magnificent, the San Callisto catacomb, and more.

The middle section of *Moment of Freedom*, "The Praiano Papers," is based on material written at around the same time as *Winter in Bellapalma*—nearly a decade earlier than the rest of the novel. In the interim between *Bellapalma* and the two works from 1966, Bjørneboe discovered Brecht. In a 1964 essay, "Ernest Hemingway and Bertolt Brecht" (a juxtaposition, perhaps, that only Bjørneboe would make), he quotes Brecht's line, "Those who laugh have simply not yet gotten the dreadful news." He continues:

> In Hemingway and Brecht, this knowledge of the "news" is obviously inborn, and forms the point of departure for the work of

---

1. Leif Longum, "Jens Bjørneboe and the Laughter of Tuscany." In *I rapporti tra Italia e Europa del nord nella letteratura e nell'arte. Giornate scandinavie 3-5 maggio 1989,* ed. Randi Langen Moen (Bologna: Universita di Bologna, 1992), 129.

both as writers; their common problem is thereby given from the first syllable: How shall one manage to live in this world at all?[2]

It appears that *Winter in Bellapalma* was a spinoff of the battle with depression recorded in "The Praiano Papers." Bjørneboe was discovering "Florentine laughter" as a tool for his own survival:

> ...this laughter is the reason why the Tuscans invented science and the clear Tuscan drawing in their cool paintings; laughter means distance. Conversely: where laughter is absent, madness begins.... the moment one takes the world with complete seriousness one is potentially insane. The whole art of learning to live means holding fast to laughter; without laughter the world is a torture chamber, a dark place where dark things will happen to us, a horror show filled with bloody deeds of violence.[3]

While Bjørneboe's early novels are not devoid of surrealistic humor, he had not yet learned to integrate "Florentine laughter" with other elements in the way that is characteristic of his later work. The comedy of *Winter in Bellapalma* and the despair of "The Praiano Papers" were kept in separate compartments, as it were.

Bellapalma shares something in common with Hemingway's sourthern European ex-patriot communities and also bears a strong resemblance to the pretty whitewashed tourist and fishing town toward the end of the "Praiano Papers." The cosmopolitan, alcoholic narrator first appears here, but in comic mode. The novel's affectionate lampooning of the Italian style of invective could be seen as a preliminary exercise for his tongue-in-cheek use of invective in his later books. The climactic showdown between the macho fisherman Tomaso and the gay ballet dancer Martin

---

2. Jens Bjørneboe, "Ernest Hemingway og Bertolt Brecht." *Om Brecht* (Oslo: Pax, 1978); *Samlede Essays: Teater* (Oslo: Pax, 1996), 329-30.

3. Jens Bjørneboe, *Moment of Freedom*, Tr. Esther Greenleaf Mürer (Chester Springs, PA: Dufour Editions, 1999), 113.

brings to mind the description of the bullfight in *Moment of Freedom*, in which "the bullfighter has danced the bull into impotence."[4]

But it is *The Bird Lovers* which *Winter in Bellapalma* prefigures most strongly. Central to both is the theme of the impact of tourism and easy money on the fabric of a community. The plot of *Winter in Bellapalma* revolves around the fishermen's demand that the town resources be diverted from building more tourist amenities to constructing a breakwater, which would improve the fishing but destroy the beach and hence the tourist trade. Since the area has been fished out and the nearest fishing grounds destroyed with dynamite, this plan is unrealistic. Here again we see an inversion of Hemingway: The fishermen's revolution loses momentum when they realize that they would have to give up their present easy life to go far out to sea in all kinds of weather. By contrast, Bjørneboe's essay on Hemingway concludes a discussion of *The Old Man and the Sea* with this comment on its author:

> No one has been further out to sea. No one has caught a bigger fish. And no one has brought less home with him.[5]

In *The Bird Lovers* the burlesque is replaced by savage satire. Bellapalma has already become a tourist town, and it is made clear that there is no way back to the status quo ante. In *The Bird Lovers* the question is whether the tourist entrepreneurs can be prevented from taking over in the first place. The deal depends on the natives' willingness to sacrifice a favorite traditional pastime—hunting and cooking songbirds—in favor of creating a bird sanctuary.

Of Hemingway's hunting Bjørneboe writes:

> …it is evident that as a rule Hemingway's sympathy is partly, and sometimes completely, on the side of the game or the bull; he identifies sometimes with the man, sometimes with the beast, but most often with both. This gives the whole an inner and distinctive

---

4. Ibid, 21-22. This description obviously owes much to Hemingway's *Death in the Afternoon*, which is discussed at length in "Hemingway and the Beasts."

5. Jens Bjørneboe, "Hemingway og dyrene," *Politi og anarki* (Oslo: Pax, 1972); *Samlede Essays: Kultur II* (Oslo: Pax, 1996), 14.

ambiguity, which I've found in no other descriptions of beast and man; they have life and death in common, and they meet there.[6]

In *The Bird Lovers* the Italians' identification with the songbirds is brought out in a surrealistic scene in which three of the characters are discussing methods of capital punishment and three others are discussing methods of cooking songbirds:

> **CARUSO**: We will have a real dinner today!
> **CAVALLI**: The electric chair is the worst in America...
> **ROSA**: So delicious.
> **CAVALLI**: In America they also use the gas chamber.
> **ROSA**: ...with white beans.
> **MARCO**: The electric chair isn't so bad. You pass out at once and...
> **PICCOLINO**: Smothered in oil and lemon and garlic. Delicious small birds.
> **FIDELE**: They jump and squirm in the chair for quite a while and it smells like burnt flesh in the room.
> **PICCOLINO**: Do you roast them on a spit, Rosa?[7]

The tourist entrepreneurs, meanwhile, turn out to be former Nazis who once occupied the village. For all their sentimental talk about "our feathered friends," the birds they identify with—as shown on their posters, and in the "Song of the Bird Lovers"—are predators:

> Birds are sweet and kind, but man is mean and full of hate.
> Anyone who kills a bird will earn a tragic fate!
>> Buzzard, kite, and vulture's kin,
>> Eagle, hawk, and peregrine![8]

The natives' desire for revenge on their former oppressors further complicates the plot, but it does not follow the expected

---

6. Ibid.

7. Jens Bjørneboe, *The Bird Lovers*, Tr. Frederick Wasser (Los Angeles: Sun & Moon Press, 1994), 35-38.

8. Ibid, 62. This quote is from an unpublished translation by Timothy H. Schiff.

trajectory. The excerpt from *Winter in Bellapalma*, "The Town Fathers Quell a Revolution," invites comparison with *The Bird Lovers'* final scene. The role played by the town priest, Father Leone, in resolving the conflict in favor of "progress" is a clear prototype of Father Piccolino's role as defense advocate for the Nazi war criminals in *The Bird Lovers*.

Bjørneboe wrote in his 1971 essay "Literature and Reality":

…we live in a world which is characterized not by *problems*, but by *dilemmas*—of problems which can't be solved. If literature brings solutions, if it brings *answers*, then it lies. With its reality-content it can only contribute to posing the questions more sharply and clearly and drastically than before.[9]

The question posed in *Winter in Bellapalma*—and still more sharply, clearly, and drastically in *The Bird Lovers*—is whether any other values, idealistic or otherwise, can stand up against economic greed. The biting pessimism and the mock-exultation with which *The Bird Lovers* ends should not obscure the empirical spirit in which Bjørneboe continually struggled to write, and which is foreshadowed here.

---

9. Jens Bjørneboe, "Litteratur og virkelighet." *Politi og Anarki* (Oslo: Pax, 1972); *Samlede Essays: Kultur I* (Oslo: Pax, 1996).

"And while we sit here waiting for the battle to begin," said one of the men to the king, "let me propose that we ask someone to tell a story—one which can pass the time without awakening heavy thoughts."

ONE

The bells in Bellapalma's old church tower awoke me in the morning. I stayed as I was, lying on my right side, carefully opened my left eye, and resolved never to drink again.

Through the cracks in the shutters the sea glittered outside, golden in the flames of the sun. Then I heard the noise of the surf.

There had been a storm in Bellapalma.

A really severe winter storm with a warm wind from Africa and ten-foot waves pounding the beach. Day and night we walked in the thunder of the surf; and especially at night, when we sat by open doors and windows among the wine bottles in Zi' Alexi's Trattoria, or walked in our shirtsleeves through the narrow cobblestone streets, the roar of the waves sounded powerfully in the darkness. If you looked out over the ocean, only an occasional stripe of foam shone white in all that black. That's how it was at night.

I closed my eyes again, but couldn't get back to sleep; I'd slept enough, and for a little while I lay there wishing I had some coffee. My glasses were gone. I got up, took my extra pair from the cupboard, and went barefoot and in my bathrobe out onto the terrace.

There wasn't a soul down on the beach, which gleamed in the sunshine. The reflections in the sea burned just as intensely as the sun itself. But the beach was dead. No seaweed, no algae, no crabs, no life. Nothing lying and rotting and smelling of the seashore. Just the too clear water, white rounded stones, and sun. There's a deathlike purity over this sandy beach, it's like a surrealistic painting. Just the beach, the horizon, and nothing.

And above sits Bellapalma, glued fast to the red cliff which rises almost vertically out of the sea. The town looks as if a child had drawn it on the mountain face with chalk.

Hearing soft steps padding up the stairs to my terrace, I turned and caught sight of Tomaso, barefoot with his pantlegs rolled midway up his tanned, muscular calves. Tomaso is a big and handsome man, but his face has a threatening aspect and many people here are afraid of him.

"Best of all fishermen," I said. "I wish you a good morning, full of peace and rest! Have you slept well?"

"Very dearest, best of all professors—have you rested well?"

Tomaso took some packs of American cigarettes out of various pockets and laid them on the table.

"You were in Naples last night?"

"Cousin Professor, what else can a poor fisherman do when he has the government against him! Not even the devil himself can put out to sea in such weather, and besides, as you know, there are hardly any fish left. To the tourists we have nothing but our sunshine to sell. May God set his curse on Bellapalma!"

He went into the living room and sat down in the armchair. He crossed his legs, and it struck me how handsomely he was dressed, with the light blue, freshly ironed shirt around his brown neck and the dark blue sweater draped like a cape over his shoulders. He wore it like a duke. Then he took off his beret and laid it on the table. His grey pants were newly pressed and spotless. His feet, his face, his hands—they were all newly washed and brown. When he lit a cigarette, the duke in him surfaced again.

"Tomaso," I said, "will you have a tiny little dram to start the day?"

And without waiting for a reply I fetched the grappa and poured some for him.

"Aren't you having one yourself?"

"I'll never drink again, Tomaso. That's a resolution."

"*Professore*, why can't you drink like a Christian, just a little? Come on, take a grappa with me!"

"In my fatherland we either drink everything in the house or nothing. It goes with the pain, Tomaso."

"You're a *bambino* in the world, Anso, in this area too you're a *bambino*. All men from the northern countries are *bambini*. Have a grappa, and I'll teach you to drink like a *cristiano*."

I took a glass, and it tore my throat like a burning cigar butt.

"*Professore*, everybody says that you were out walking around the city in your pajamas last night."

"Yes, Tomaso, I felt a need for company. The others here have girlfriends, I'm the only one who doesn't, because I'm fat and melancholy and have glasses and not much hair."

"You were at Alexi's in that get-up, and you carried your pajama top slung over your shoulders like a hussar's jacket. That doesn't do for a personage like you."

"No one has ever understood me, Tomaso. Are you starting in now too?"

"Very dearest *professore*, there's something I've been thinking about."

"Yes?"

"It isn't true what they say!"

"No?"

"You aren't crazy. You're just very nervous."

"What?"

"You aren't crazy—just *molto nervoso*."

"That's right, Tomaso, I'm very nervous. That's why I go out at night like that to look for human companionship."

"You were up on the piazza too, *professore*, and wanted to drive to Gransole in your car. But you didn't have the keys in your pajamas, so you got very mad and *rabbiato* and started wrestling with Mario. People say that your whole body is hairy as a wolf."

"Is it necessary to tell me everything, Tomaso?"

"Is it true, *professore*, that you're so hairy?"

"In my fatherland all intellectuals are as hairy as wolves, and that business of going out at night in our pajamas is just a habit we've gotten into. In the winter it's often very cold."

"The Northmen are very great fishermen," said Tomaso. "They're like devils on the sea, and catch stockfish worth hundreds of thousands of lire in a day. Vittorio has fished in the North Sea, and he told me about it. The Norwegian fishermen are all very grand *signori* compared with us Italian fishermen, who are poor tiny little lice and are hated by the government and might as well go off and die. In Italy a fisherman is as despised as a dead dog."

We had another grappa.

"The North Sea must be very terrible," he said thoughtfully, "but still there are fish in it. It's supposed to be very frightening, gray as lead, with huge waves and freezing cold, and with no sun at all."

For a while he sat silent and dark before speaking again:

"*Professore?*"

"Yes?"

"I've never spoken with an Italian *professore*. In Italy the best people don't want to talk with anything so paltry as a fisherman. But you, *professore*, you're a good person, and for you there's no difference between people on this earth. I will always be friends with you. And you say hello to all the fishermen and to Cesare too, even if he's a tramp and a bum. You don't make any distinctions. And I'll see that you never go alone to Naples."

"It's true that I like to greet people," I said. "I learned that in my own country. Especially out in the countryside people greet everybody and wish them good rest or good work. It's quite natural."

"Do the rich do it too?"

"In the countryside everybody says hello."

"The rich in Italy haven't learned to greet people. They just go around in their pointed shoes and their hair-oil and stick their noses in the air. They're bad people, *professore*! They won't even look at a fisherman. They're miserable people. God damn them!"

"But the duke says hello!"

"Yes, the duke greets everybody. But he comes from a fine old family, so he must have learned it at home."

"It's just the ones who have gotten rich since the war who don't know that you're supposed to say hello, Tomaso. And that's their misfortune."

"And the tourists! Best of all *professori*, the tourists are very stuck-up people, and they don't say hello. They are cold and evil people, and they despise the fishermen."

"And Father Leone says hello!"

"Yes, *monsignore* greets all of us, if he isn't drunk. When he's drunk he doesn't greet anybody, but that's because he can't see, not because he has a hard and arrogant heart. *Monsignore* is a good man too, he's a humble man. Especially when he's been drunk for several days and then sobers up, he's a humble and good person who comes down to the beach and talks with the fishermen."

Tomaso sat silent for a while, and his face changed expression and grew dark again. Then he said:

"I hate tourists. They've spoiled everything for us fishermen here. They're miserable people. Likewise Mr. Georg and Mr. Arnold are bad men who don't say hello. I don't like you to associate with them, *professore*."

He raised himself halfway out of his chair and drew something from his back pocket. Then he sat down again and unpacked it carefully from several layers of paper.

"*Buonissimo professore*, I must ask you a favor. Will you read this for me? O Madonna, I'm a poor wretch of a fisherman!"

He handed me a postcard, and proceeded to explain:

"It isn't that my reason is poor, but I've never learned. I have a very good brain, but my father died when I was five years old, and by the time I was eight I was doing road work. Please read it for me, *professore*!"

The card was postmarked from Holland and contained a couple of sentences in Italian. A greeting, and the information that the sender would arrive in Bellapalma in March. He looked happy.

"Is she the one you talk to in the spring, best of all fishermen?"

"Yes, she comes every spring, and she's going to buy me a fishnet this year."

"And then there's one coming in the summer and one in the fall?"

"Two in the summer, *professore*; one leaves at the end of June, and the other comes at the beginning of July."

He got up and thanked me for the grappa, and I saw him out to the terrace.

"*Salve*, Tomaso! Have a good rest!"

He gave me an iron handshake, padded down the stairs and vanished into the little street which goes down to the beach. I went into the big bedroom with the double bed, took off my pajamas and put on some pants, a shirt, and tennis shoes, though it was pleasant to stand barefoot on the tile floor. Then I went out onto the terrace, down the steps and on down the narrow, steep street. I went straight across the beach toward the town.

The waves were no longer so big, not more than a yard high, and no fisherman in Northern Europe would have dreamed of staying home because of them. There wasn't a hint of a breeze on the sea, and the surface was like glass, just light and sunshine.

Altogether a dead and dull mood lay over the town. No one had been out to sea for two or three weeks because there was either scirocco or waves. The town lay there, warm and damp and musty. A wind from Africa, winter, no tourists, no fishing, nothing. A strange stillness and lack of motion which had nothing to do with peace. It was a time of waiting, a long, silent crisis. I wasn't the only one who had cut loose last night.

Then I met Cesare, bent, thin and old.

We went into Alexi's and ordered a can of wine. The place was already full, and it was past ten o'clock. People were playing cards, smoking, and drinking. There was no great merriment, only a couple laughed when they saw me, but they all greeted me politely. They were mostly fishermen.

Carola brought me my spectacles along with the wine. "You left them here yesterday, *professore*. It wasn't us who broke them. You must have cracked them on the stairs up at the piazza. Poor *professore!*"

I stuck them in my pocket and poured some wine for Cesare and myself. I raised my glass in a toast: "Life is hard!"

"Ever onward!" answered Cesare.

Then we drank.

"You're smart to have two pairs of glasses," he said. "If you break one pair, then you can just get out the other and use it. It's very clever of you to arrange it like that."

With the great drinker's self-discipline he rapidly drank two glasses one after the other, and wouldn't have any more.

"You work too hard," said Cesare. "Everybody knows that you work like a madman. People can hear the clatter of your typewriter until late at night, and in the morning you sit on the terrace and go on writing. Won't the sun rise without your help?"

"No, Cesare, the sun is in a very bad way. Good appetite!"

"Good appetite, *professore!*"

Further up the street I met the police chief, *signor* Agnolino. He was not in uniform but tottered around in duck trousers with a piece of bread in his hand, ancient as he was.

He has light blue eyes, a white mustache, and red cheeks. His white hair is close-cropped and his shoulders thin and rounded. The hand with the crust of bread was brown, wrinkled, and gnarled. He was on the way to Alexi's for a glass of wine to go with the bread. Agnolino means "little lamb."

"*Professore,* think about the eternal things while you are young!"

Chief Agnolino is a pious old man who has preserved his youthful power for a long time; everybody knows that he has a girlfriend thirty-five years younger than himself.

We took our leave, and I went on. On the stairs I had a bit of luck. I met The Girl.

I don't know who she is or what her name is. I don't even know what country she's from. But this was the first time I had met her alone. She's very young, probably a little over twenty.

I had met her often in the company of a lady who was older and very tailored. The tailored lady was probably about my own age, and they looked as if they were completely wrapped up in each other, so

I never dared say hello to them. But now The Girl was approaching by herself, and I didn't know what to do, I started worrying that either to say hello or not to—either one was wrong. But we met alone on the stairs, and I got very nervous. She was wearing tennis shoes and jeans and had a sweater over her shoulder. I thought I'd better do something halfway between greeting and not greeting, so she could take it however she chose. As she drew near me my throat tensed so that I couldn't say a thing, I just moved my head slightly and made a sort of groan. Then I saw a blush spread over her face, and she smiled, but I was much too anxious to smile back. I just looked stern. But I knew that a blush had gone through her, and my heart started pounding so that I could see it outside my shirt, and my fingers went numb. When she had gone on down the stairs I leaned against the wall to catch my breath. I'd seen her every day for six weeks now, and this was the first time we had greeted each other. But I knew every feature of her face, every lock of her hair. Now and then she and her friend eat at Alexi's. There I've learned her by heart.

"Lord, what a vain old fool you are!" I said to myself. But it didn't help. I took off my reserve glasses and polished them so that no one would see that I was standing there being happy. I was very happy that I had greeted The Girl.

"If it goes on like this, you'll be able to speak to her in three years," I said to make fun of myself. But I didn't let myself be squelched. I felt happy, and I was humming a little song when I reached the piazza, where Mario was standing behind the bar. He was alone, and he was singing too, a mournful folksong about amore.

"Cut out your wailing, Mario, and do your duty!"

"Good morning, *professore*! Did you sleep well? And how are you feeling?"

"Like a dead dog, Mario. I feel rotten. Give me a beer, O best of all waiters!"

He opened a beer:

"Dogs don't drink beer in the morning, least of all dead dogs. Do you want something for a headache too?"

"To drink beer in the morning is reserved for people, Mario. The living, one must note."

"One day we'll all be under the ground, *professore*, and it'll be very boring, because then there won't be any more beer."

"Can't you talk about something more pleasant, Mario?"

But I was happy and couldn't forget that I had greeted The Girl and that she had blushed. Besides, the beer worked wonders, and I sat down at a table so as to be alone and think about her. She had smiled, and I repeated my nod several times as I sat there. Maybe it hadn't been such a flop after all, and I pictured The Girl as she smiled.

Now I had to think up a couple of sentences which I could say at a future meeting.

The sun had reached the piazza, and I sat as if in a room surrounded by whitewashed walls on all sides, but with the blue sky above me. Here there are three bars: the Sunshine, where Mario stands behind the counter, and two others: Peppino's and the Sport. We always go to the Sunshine. There's no motor road to the piazza, technologically it's just as virginal as it was two hundred years ago—for the fact is, neither cars nor motorcycles can drive on stairs or in streets which are as steep as Bellapalma's. All motor vehicles must park on the highway above the town, and everything must be carried down on foot. So it's a common job here to be a porter. Only rarely do you see donkeys in the streets.

As I sat there a steady but thin stream of porters and laborers passed by; they went single file straight across the Piazza del Sole, which is the square's full name. Every two or three minutes one of them would emerge from behind the corner to my right, cross the piazza and disappear on the other side, in the direction of the beach. They were all barefoot, wearing rolled-up khakis and thin shirts or sleeveless undershirts; each had half of a burlap sack tied around his forehead and over his head, so that it hung down over his shoulders and back. Each of the laborers carried a basket of stones on his back, and the porters carried food, wine, and whatever else needed to be taken down to the houses and restaurants by the sea. Common to them all was the strained expression on their faces, their bare feet, and the much too heavy burdens which they bore. The workmen had a layer of chalky dust over their brown shoulders and hands. Behind them, at one of the other bars, a party of Italian tourists was having breakfast, three gentlemen with shiny pomaded hair, tight pants and pointed shoes, along with two blonde girls. They belonged to that part of the Italian populace who don't say hello to Tomaso, and the tight pants were striking. Certain Italian men are probably the only ones in the world who are proud of their rumps. All the while the thin line of laborers filed past them, and the bowed heads under the baskets of rock gave them a strange look of almost antique humility.

Mario was now sweeping the piazza outside the Sunshine, he set tables, moved chairs, and with rolling eyes and puckered lips took up his song again:

> "The very nicest thing I know
> Is love, is love. . . !
> The very loveliest thing I know
> Is lo-o-o-o-ve, ohhh!"

I knew some of the laborers, had drunk beer with them now and then, and now sat there greeting them. Despite the uncomfortable position of their heads under the baskets, there wasn't one of them who didn't smile and wave and say a couple of words in return. Mario continued:

". . . is lo-o-o-ove. . .oh!"

Then Georg and Martin came around the corner—Georg first, walking fast, Martin after him with both his miniature pinschers on a leash. He has a special leash for them, a leather strap which divides in two at the bottom so that it can be fastened to both collars. It doesn't give the dogs much freedom, and they must always walk side by side. Georg looked at Mario, cocked his head and said:

"Tread softly, Martin, this is high poesy! Morning, Mario!"

Mario was behind the bar again like lightning:

"Good morning, *signori*! Did the gentlemen sleep well?"

"Like two pebbles on the beach," replied Georg, "the night was lovely, Mario, but the morning was terrible. This morning we quarreled. Martin is in an abominable humor."

Georg is red-haired, with a dark, brownish-red color on his face and neck, the wholesome weather-bitten color which comes from wine.

With concern Mario fixed his big coal-black eyes on Martin's young face:

"Is it true? Has something been troubling you?"

Martin pinched his lips together before replying:

"Don't you think that I could just as well get some new pants? God, but I'm so tired of the ones I have!"

"Everything becomes you," said Mario with feeling. "You're slim as an eel around the hips. And the pants you have on fit splendidly."

Martin said:

"You have no idea how tired I am of them. These pants I'm wearing are absolutely the best-fitting ones of all, but they wrinkle around the waist."

Martin stepped out into the space between the tables and raised his arms, turning around so that Mario could see him from all sides.

"See, Mario? They wrinkle! Can you see it? So you can imagine how the others are!"

Now Martin turned to Georg and spoke to him:

"There, you hear! Mario also thinks that they're a miserable fit around the waist!"

Meanwhile Georg had got his morning beer; he emptied the bottle in two swigs and became more affable.

"Yes, yes," he said amiably, "we'll go to the tailor afterwards, then."

Martin's face lit up.

"Oh, Georg!" he said, "Thank you!"

Mario set the freshly-made coffee on the counter and produced two Danish pastries, while Martin went on:

"Oh, I'm so thrilled, Georgie-Porgie! What color shall we get, then?"

Another workman crossed the piazza; he was old and dried by the wind, and the calloused soles of his feet dragged against the cement. It was Camillo, and he smiled at me toothlessly. I pointed at my beer bottle and looked at him questioningly.

"Another time, *signore*!"

"We'll look at fabric up at the tailor's," said Georg to Martin. And to Mario he continued: "Did something happen last night?"

"They caught a smuggler early this morning up on the road. He was coming from Naples."

"A boy from this town?"

"He's from here, yes, but he isn't a boy anymore. He's in his fifties. It's Francesco. He used to be a fisherman."

"He was with someone, you said?"

"Are you thinking of anyone in particular, *signore*?"

"Well, Tomaso, for instance? Isn't that his name?"

"What color do you think I should get, Mario?" said Martin. "They have a lovely velvet in dark red. But maybe blue would be prettier for pants?"

"He isn't the first one to take up smuggling instead of fishing," said Georg. "He has a wife and children? Francesco, I mean?"

"Four children," mumbled Mario. "They claim that the fishing has gotten so bad that it doesn't pay anymore."

"So I'll take blue, then!" said Martin. "Light blue! And we'll make them in exactly the same cut as fishermen's pants, but in velvet instead! Right, Georg? Then I'll look like a fisherboy!"

Without batting an eyelash Georg replied:

"You'll be the world's sweetest fisherboy. You'll be a dream!"

"Do you think?"

"A dream boy!"

Another workman crossed the square. I didn't know him, and right afterwards came another one. Martin turned and looked after them.

"God," he said, "I get so nervous with all those men going past all the time. The place is crawling with them! What on earth are they doing?"

"You shouldn't get so upset about it," said Georg. "They're just carrying a little rock."

"But why? Are they going to keep it up all day?"

"Carrying rock is something poor people do to pass the time. They can keep it up for weeks. They're indefatigable."

Now Martin got mad.

"That's not what I meant! I'm not as dumb as you think! They must be building houses! Aren't they, Mario?"

"That's right," said Mario, "they're building houses for the tourists. Every year we put up new houses which can be rented out during the season, so we're always getting room for more guests. After all, there's not much room here in the town, and the beach isn't being fully used. We have the finest bathing beach along this whole coast."

"What kind of people are they? What did they do before you started all this building?" said Georg.

"They were fishermen. All of them were fishermen."

Then Martin caught sight of me, and came over and offered his hand.

"So nice to find you here, Anso! We were afraid that you'd banged yourself up so badly that you'd have to stay in bed today. We'd been thinking about going down to see you afterwards."

When Martin is like that, he has both warmth and friendliness to give. He's like a good nurse. Then I heard Georg's laughter. He had also spotted me, and now left the bar and came over to my table.

"You set a new Bellapalma record in falling downstairs last night," he said. "I actually think you rolled from the town hall all the way down to the beach. That means you fell for about ten minutes without stopping. How was the trip down?"

"Just awful, thanks," I said.

"You came literally rolling onto the piazza here, and you were amazingly lightly clad considering the season and the hour. But you got up as soon as you'd rolled to a stop. It was only later that you fell down again on the other side of the square."

"Can't you find something more pleasant to talk about?" I said.

"Did you hurt yourself?" said Martin.

"I broke my glasses," I replied, "and I have some black-and-blue marks and my wrist is a bit stiff, but it's nothing worth mentioning."

"Come have some cognac," said Georg. "It heals all wounds."

"No thanks," I said. "I'd like to sit here a while without talking. But ask Mario to bring me a *caffè latte*."

They went back to the bar, and then it was that Tomaso came onto the piazza, across it and over to the Sunshine. He was wearing black pants now, and black pointed shoes on his feet, and it struck me how dark he looked compared to the blond Martin and the red-haired Georg. Tomaso seemed utterly rough-hewn beside them: the coal-black hair over the low forehead, the black, piercing eyes, the strong lower jaw and the hard, craggy features gave his dark-brown face a threatening, gloomy expression. Silent and closed in, he took a place at the bar and cast a quick sidelong glance at the other two. Then he drew his black, bushy eyebrows together into one thick line. I've never understood what dwells at the bottom of him. As far as I know I'm the only one he's friendly with. Today he looked even foxier than usual. With a cigarette in the corner of his mouth and with half-closed eyes he continued to inspect Martin and Georg. He ordered a coffee with brandy in it from Mario.

"Good morning," said Georg.

Tomaso did not reply, but continued to stare at them for a while and then rapidly said a few unintelligible words to Mario.

"What's he saying?" asked Georg.

Mario blushed and looked unhappy: "I can't repeat it to you."

"Yes, say it! I'm interested!"

"It was an insult, *signore*."

Contemptuously Tomaso half turned his back to them and pretended not to hear the conversation. Martin was pink and took a couple of steps out onto the floor.

"Can't we go to the tailor now?" he said loudly.

Georg hauled himself up onto one of the bar stools and turned toward him.

"You can go now, I'll be along in a while. I want to know what he said. Mario, if you don't tell me I'll never set foot in the Sunshine again! Say it!"

First Mario looked cautiously at Martin, then he cleared his throat a couple of times. He was rather desperate.

"'He said that you bring shame on your mother by going around with a boy who resembles a girl.'"

"I don't want to stay here any longer!" said Martin.

"Does everybody see us like that?" continued Georg.

"No," replied Mario in a friendly tone, "most of them are aware how much the tourists mean for the town."

"That was beautifully said," replied Georg. "Give me another glass, please."

"This is an awfully bad habit," said Georg. "Give me another glass, please."

Footsteps sounded on the piazza, and Arnold, Pamela and Marie came practically bounding over to us. They were gay and cheerful. Pamela shouted out the news:

"God, have you heard that Pietro and Paolo caught two smugglers last night?!"

"Goodness, it's nice to see you!" said Martin, stroking back his much too long, silky-fine hair.

"Only one smuggler," replied Georg. "They only got hold of one of them in the dark."

"Is that so!" cried Pamela and looked around delightedly. "So the other one is still at large! Mario, you know everything that goes on! How exciting that they caught the smuggler yesterday! But what's become of the other? Who was the other smuggler?"

Tomaso turned his head slowly and looked at them over his shoulder.

"Who was the other one, Mario? Out with it!"

Pamela was dreadfully excited, and Mario raised his arms above his head and opened his eyes wide.

"I have no idea, *signora*! How can I? Nobody tells me anything!"

He was a picture of persecuted and unjustly suspected innocence. Arnold ordered three fruit juices, three coffees and three Danish pastries.

"God!" shrieked Pamela. "But I've completely forgotten to give you your morning kisses! Arnold has had his already."

She kissed Georg on the mouth, then turned toward Martin and grabbed him by the shoulders. He twisted away.

"Yecch!" he said, "don't be so disgusting!"

Then we heard Tomaso's voice, loud and clear:

"Sancta Maria! Full of grace and mercy! Holy mother of God!"

Thereupon he addressed a number of rapid and unintelligible words to Mario, and turned away again. It was utterly silent in the bar for a moment. Then Arnold spoke:

"What the hell did he say?"

"It was in dialect," said Georg. "I didn't understand."

"What did he say, Mario?" yelled Arnold; he was angry.

"It cannot be repeated when there are ladies present."

"Mario too must have his morning kiss!" cried Pamela. "Here, Mario!"

And she kissed him across the bar while he was setting out the fruit juice and coffee. Arnold's handsome, manly face had turned red with fury.

"What—did—he—say,—Mario?"

Now Mario looked as if he wanted to run away.

"Just say it, Mario," said Georg. "The little girls can stand to hear it."

"Hm," said Mario and looked down, "he said that your women behave like little dogs do on the street, and that people must keep their children inside so that they won't see it and have their souls corrupted!"

Arnold turned toward Tomaso, and he is a tall and vigorous man, just a little over forty, so he looked quite dangerous.

"What the hell do you mean by that?!" he yelled, so loudly that the tourists over at the other bar jumped in their seats.

"Calm down," said Georg. "I think it's crystal clear what he means."

"What do you mean?" repeated Arnold somewhat more softly.

Marie put her arms around him and kissed him on the neck:

"Take it easy, Arnold! Oh, be careful! He can be dangerous."

"I don't give a damn," said Arnold and drank down his fruit juice, making a face as if he were biting the head off a toad. "He has insulted you! Give me a cognac, Mario!"

"He has only expressed his opinion," said Georg, "which in this case means the people's opinion, and that, as you know, is God's opinion. Martin and I also got ours from him just before you came. And it's a rare opportunity to learn something that money can't buy. That's practically the only thing you can't get for cash in Bellapalma."

"You're just a coward," said Arnold.

"Yes," said Georg, "that too. I'm cowardly as hell."

"What did he say to you?"

Georg replied with a glance at Martin:

"You can just imagine."

At the same moment Pamela spotted me sitting behind the door.

"God!" she cried. "There's Anso over there! He survived! He too shall have his kiss!" They all turned to look at me, with the exception of Tomaso, while she came over and kissed me lingeringly. It didn't taste too bad, but actually I was sitting and thinking of The Girl. On Tomaso's back I could read what he was thinking:

"This is a most dreadful woman, *professore*. She is *terribilissima*!"

"Okay," said Arnold to Georg, "so this Tomaso insulted Martin too!"

Pamela looked at Tomaso with half-closed eyes and said softly:

"Do you think he's dangerous? I do. His eyes are like diamonds."

She stood still for a moment, then went on slowly and dreamily:

"They must use knives here—"

Arnold looked with interest at Mario:

"Do they?"

"It happens rather seldom, *signore*, and mostly when women are involved."

"I don't know what you mean by *seldom*, Mario," said Georg, "but in the next town there were two murders for jealousy in six months when I was here last year."

"Okay, now I'm going to the tailor's!" said Martin. "Pamela and Marie, come along and look at fabrics! I'm getting some pants made."

"All right," said Pamela, putting her arm around Marie. But they went on standing there. Georg ordered a martini, and Arnold a cognac.

"Then Arnold must go to the tailor's too," said Marie.

"I'm coming," said he, "but first I want to hear about the stabbings. Had somebody seduced their wives?"

There came a long, hollow groan from Tomaso:

"Ave Maria! Full of grace and forgiveness!"

"Now he's starting in again!" said Pamela, transported.

"What had they done to their wives?" Arnold persisted.

"No, it's not like that at all," said Georg. "One of the murderers said in court that he stabbed the man because he had looked at his sister on the street as if she were a bad woman."

That impressed Arnold, and he said inquiringly to Mario:

"Is that true?"

"Yes, that's right," said Mario, "people really frown on that sort of thing here."

"Hell's bells," said Arnold, putting a hand to his head. "And the other one? Had he only looked too?"

"No," said Georg, "he had spoken to and walked with a girl who was engaged. The fiancé took a knife to him right afterwards."

"Lord help us! And neither of them had touched the girls?"

Once more Tomaso turned and spoke to Mario, rapidly and angrily, in heavy dialect. Then he turned his back again.

"Just translate him," said Arnold. "These are interesting points of view. What did he say?"

"He was speaking about you, *signore*."

"And what did he say, Mario?"

"He said that you are a wicked and unchaste man, and that everybody knows that you're living lustfully with two women without being married to them. He says that it disgraces the women of Bellapalma to be forced to see such a thing."

"That was quite a lot," said Arnold, and stood up. "Come on, let's go to the tailor's, and afterwards we'll go for a swim. Tomaso, you are a very charming man, a splendid person!"

Pamela looked at the fisherman, her spine wilting, her gaze glassy:

"He's beautiful," she said. "He is the handsomest man in Bellapalma!"

"Let's go!" cried Martin. "I'm going to the tailor's. Come on!"

Everybody got up except Georg, who remained seated and said:

"I'm not finished yet, Martin. I'll have another glass first, then I'll be along."

They went off toward the corner. Martin turned back to Georg:

"What swimming trunks should I wear? The blue or the green?"

"Take the blue ones," said Georg. "You're so bewitching in them."

Then they left, and as they rounded the corner they met a laborer with a basket of stones on his neck.

"Frightful social conditions," I heard Arnold say to Marie as they disappeared from view. The workman was old Camillo, on a new trip. He smiled and waved, but declined my offer of beer.

Then a large party of tourists came into the piazza, evidently a busload which had stopped for a couple of hours to look at our little town about which so many interesting things are told.

"A dry martini, Mario!" called Georg, "but with more gin in it. Just a little vermouth on the top!"

I sat there watching the tour group being chased across the piazza by the leader. There was something about these tourists which I didn't understand; their faces were pinky-white, like marzipan pigs, and shapeless, almost without features. Many of them were large and rather fat, and the blandness and impassivity of their faces made them resemble great big three-year-olds. Only slowly did it dawn on me that the new arrivals must be Scandinavian or Dutch. A very tall gentleman with lemon-yellow hair was sweating profusely and carried a copy of *Stockholmstidningen* in his hand. The paper was folded open to the comics. He was wearing a short-sleeved child's shirt with a flowered pattern. His fat arms were white and freckled. The tour guide drove the company across the square with loud shouts, but the large gentleman had discovered Peppino's Bar and put up a resistance. He wanted cognac and Ramlösa, he cried, and several of the company took his part. Peppino himself had dashed out into the street, and was now blocking their way down to the beach. He bowed and smiled and nudged them in toward the bar. Many of the travelers sided with the rebel leader in the flowered shirt, and called out loudly what they would have; some wanted milk and others wanted soft drinks. The large gentleman ordered three whiskeys-and-soda from Peppino, and a moment later the tour guide was out of the game. Everybody swooped down on the sidewalk tables and called out their orders. One lady wanted milk and sweet rolls. They looked like a nursery school of albinos on an outing. The tour guide followed after Peppino, fussing and forcing the party to eat and drink in a hurry.

I looked over at Mario and Georg. Both sat staring hard at the newcomers. Georg had got his second martini, but hadn't touched it.

"They're Germans," I said. "There you can see how you people look!"

He didn't reply, but slowly turned and picked up his glass.

A skinny lady with something alcohol-free in her hand stood up, then lifted her other arm and pointed at me.

"God!" she shrieked. "It's him!"

A couple of the others began looking at me too. Then she walked resolutely across the square and over to my table. She spoke Norwegian:

"I recognized you at once!" said she. "You are Hans Berlow! I've seen pictures of you!"

"*Buonissima Signora*," I said, "*non capisco!*"

"Ha, ha!" she said. "You rascal!"

"*Ma veramente! Non capisco inglese!*"

"Nonsense!" she said and sat down. "You can't fool me! But anyway, you're better looking in your pictures. Is it only lately you've gotten like this?"

"How's that?" I said. "What do you mean by 'like this'?"

"Well," she said, "in the pictures you have more hair, and besides you're not wearing glasses. And you're not corpulent in the photographs. And naturally one can't see that your face is red, either."

"Was that all?" I said.

"No," she said. "Then of course the thing with your lower lip!"

"Oh?" I said, "you've noticed the thing with my lower lip?"

"Of course! Any child can see that."

She ruminated in silence for a bit. Then she went on:

"You mustn't take it amiss if I say it straight out, Berlow. But the surgeons have gotten so clever since the last war. And I'm sure that you could have something done about your lower lip. It might be only a couple of stitches."

"Now you just listen to me," I said. "There are lots of women who like me just fine, even if I'm a bit overweight and have something wrong with my lip. And that's because I have such a stormy and passionate disposition!"

I stared at her, rolling my eyes.

"Hm," she said, "that doesn't make much of an impression."

"Aha," I said, "I can tell you that I'm extremely passionate. When I'm in Naples I go to the museum every single night!"

"If I were you," she said after a pause, "I would still get something done about your lip."

"You think it's essential?" I asked.

"Yes," she said. "And then the matter of your weight. I think you eat too much—or, or does it perhaps come from drink?"

"Yes," I said, "certainly it all comes from drink, because I hardly ever eat. Once I really did look the way I do in the pictures, but now I've drunk so much that it's turned my hair completely red, and I've lost a lot of hair too, and have gotten very nearsighted besides. One time I drank so much wine that I almost went blind, and the worst thing was that I lost my hearing as well, and got a rash all over my body. Then came the thing with my lower lip— and yes, the color of my face too, of course. It's all due to drink."

The party of tourists was beginning to move, and a lady called to her. She got up.

"Adieu," she said, "we have to leave now. I hope you're not angry because I'm going? My whole family are teetotalers."

"Yes," I said. "I'm just miserable knowing that I won't get to see you anymore."

"You're just saying that," she said.

"No," I said, "I'm telling the truth. You have really made me rather depressed."

Then she went with the tour group over the piazza and down the stairs which led to the beach with all the beautiful, newly-painted boats on it.

I went over to the bar, where Georg was still sitting, for I had started thinking that of course the thing with The Girl was hopeless, and that surely I had just looked dumb and ridiculous when I met her on the stairs. In fact she hadn't been smiling at me, but *laughing* at me, and it would just be stupid to sit here thinking up a sentence I could use to make her blush the next time we met. If she had blushed to begin with, it was surely from the need to suppress her laughter. None of this was the least bit fun to sit and think about, so now I would rather talk with Georg. All my joy and pride over The Girl was gone. She was so pretty too, and everything was meaningless.

"What did you say his name was, that fisherman they caught last night?" said Georg to Mario.

"Francesco," he replied.

That was when I discovered that Tomaso too was gone.

"Oh yes," said Georg, "I've seen him with his nets down on the beach. By the way, have you heard any more about this deviltry the fishermen are cooking up?"

Mario grew very grave:

"I only know that there's been unrest among them for several days, and that Tomaso is talking to them all the time. People say he's stirring them up."

"Stirring them up?"

"Yes, inciting them. There's an old issue that he's dragged out again, he says that they should build a breakwater outside the beach and create a proper harbor, so that it will be possible to go out and fish in bad weather. That's when the fishing is best, he says."

"That sounds reasonable."

"It would destroy the bathing beach for the tourists."

"But surely the fishing is more important?"

"Oh, no! The tourists are much more important to the town than the fishing is. The sea is almost fished out here, and the tourists bring in nearly everything we have to live on."

"All right, I understand. Tomaso is inciting the fishermen. He's a troublemaker."

"Yes, precisely, *signore*! He is a bad man, an evil person who wants to spoil things for all of us. What in the world would Bellapalma be without the tourists?! An ordinary poor village!"

Just then Marie and Pamela and Arnold came into view at the other end of the square, eager, elated and breathless. They waved at us.

"Georg and Hans!" called Pamela, "you must come with us. Something's going on down at the beach. The fishermen are making trouble!"

Georg got up:

"What's that?"

"It's the fishermen," Arnold shouted back. "They're holding a meeting and saying that they want to convert the beach into a harbor. The workmen are going to construct a breakwater instead of building more tourist houses! They're holding a meeting down by their boats! We're going down to listen to them!"

"This could be interesting," said Georg. "I'll come up again afterwards, Mario. Are you coming, Anso?"

"No," I said, "not now."

When Georg had gone, Tomaso came back. He was coming from the beach, and they must have met him on their way down.

"Very dearest *professore*!"

"Best of all *pescatori*!"

"What have you got?" said Mario, looking at him eagerly.

"Lucky Strike, Camel, Chesterfield," replied Tomaso.

"How much?"

"Most excellent Mario! For the time being you can have twenty cartons of Chesterfields, ten of Luckies, and ten of Camels, at the usual price."

"That's all, Tomaso?"

"*Carissimo* Mario, I'm having a lot of trouble with the transport just now. Those two bloodhounds Pietro and Paolo are very bad people who are watching every step I take. These loathsome Neapolitans are a disgrace to the mothers who brought them into the world! You'll get more later."

"Fine. Will you put them in the garden?"

"They're sitting there already, packed as usual."

"*Bravissimo pescatore*!" I said. "They caught Francesco last night. You didn't tell me that! Have they got anything on him?"

"No," said Tomaso, "he wasn't carrying anything. They'll have to let him out again today. Do you have the money, most excellent Mario?"

"You'll get it this afternoon, cousin Tomaso!"

"Well," said Tomaso, "I'm going down to the beach. Good appetite and good rest, *professore*!"

"Listen," I said, "you mustn't give in on the breakwater. It's a shame for all of Italy how they treat the fishermen here. A harbor is the least you have a right to. And remember, the town treasury will pay!"

"*Carissimo professore*, you are a good person, who stands on our side and understands that fishermen too are human beings with a right to respect and love. You were already greeting me before we got acquainted! Now everything's going according to your plan."

He turned and crossed the square in the direction of the stairs leading down to the beach. At the same instant the policemen came around the corner from above, in uniform and heavily armed. They greeted Mario and me.

"Good day, *signori*, good appetite!"

"Good day, bravest of all *carabinieri*!"

Pietro caught sight of Tomaso, who was just coming to the stairs.

"We'll get you too, soon!" he yelled.

Tomaso turned in fury. Sparks flew from him, and he bared his teeth, two gleaming, flawless rows which had never seen a dentist.

"I don't know what you're talking about," he snarled. "You have no respect for a poor honest fisherman. Pretty soon nobody but the loathsome uniformed bastards of certain Neapolitans will be allowed to live in Italy, this wretched country. Why should you arrest me?"

"We almost took you last night," rejoined Pietro. "Next time it'll be your turn."

Tomaso's face turned black with rage:

"What have I done wrong? Is it forbidden to be a fisherman? Why should you arrest me? O Madonna, what evil people you are to talk like that! Why was I born in a country where I have the government against me, and where the most evil people have the power? You, Pietro, have always been an evil and cold man, whose stony heart brings shame over your mother!"

Tomaso turned and went down the stairs, and we could hear him muttering and cursing to himself. Paolo leaned across the bar:

"Have you got any good cigarettes, Mario?"

"Yes," replied Mario, "I just happen to have a few packs which an American gave me as a present. There's Lucky Strike and Chesterfield. I don't have any Camels at the moment. What will you have?"

"Lucky Strike," said Paolo.

"Same here!" said Pietro, and put down his gun on the table.

"Most excellent, highly *brave carabinieri*," I said, "without men like you the fatherland would sink into crime and lawlessness! It would lose its colonies."

"Yes," said Pietro and looked at me, "that's the way it is, but most people in this exceedingly miserable town, they don't understand that, and call us maggots and parasites on society. But you, *professore*, are a well-read and educated man, so you understand it. My friend and honored colleague Paolo and myself, we are not just courageous, we are also highly intelligent men."

"Yes," I replied, "you are *molto intelligenti.*"

Paolo nodded in confirmation.

"Please," said Mario, "here are two packs apiece. They're a gift, and cost nothing. Tomaso is an evil man who wants to destroy our society and drive the tourists away."

The two *carabinieri* each took a coffee with a dram in it, and we stood for a while and talked about the English queen, in whom both were intensely interested.

"I wish I was an Englishman," said Paolo. "Then maybe I'd have been a general by now, and be talking with the Queen every day."

"I know where Oslo is," said Mario, "because I've always collected stamps, and three years ago a Norwegian *signore* was living here, a *grandissimo pittore* who painted the most beautiful pictures of little flowers. He was living at Giuseppe's, and got delirium from being here, but before he got sick he was always trading stamps for cognac, and he drew a map and showed me where Oslo was. He was a highly intelligent gentleman."

"Then I'd have made Pietro a colonel," Paolo went on. "If I'd been an English general."

Pietro rolled his eyes wildly and said that if he had been a colonel in the English army, then he would have married a blond girl and had lots of *bambini* with her.

"Paolo, maybe *you* know where Oslo is!" said Mario.

"I'm not a stamp collector," said Paolo, "so I don't need to know that. But I've learned the art of reading, so someday I can find out, because my uncle in Naples has a big book with pictures of all the countries in the world."

A wild, piercing shriek sounded over the piazza. It was the boy Beniamino, who was standing by the stairs waving his arms.

"Pietro and Paolo!" he yelled. "You must come at once! Oh, immediately! There's a fight on the beach! Oh, a terrible fight, and there's been an accident with the one gentleman!"

Pietro and Paolo and I set off at a bound, and Mario had no more thought for his bar, but followed after us. We ran down the stairs and raced at full speed through the narrow street which bears the name "Via dei naviganti"—Seamen's Street. It goes straight down to the beach.

TWO

An hour later an oppressive silence and the smell of iodine reigned on the terrace outside Arnold's apartment. Right below the terrace itself lies an orange grove and a small vineyard, both rarities in Bellapalma, where there is hardly any earth to set a plant in. Leading into the apartment is a huge arched glass door, which almost always stands open.

I sat on the antique marble bench on the terrace and polished my spectacles while I waited for the others to come out. When I heard them, I put down my glasses on the table next to the iodine and the band-aids.

Arnold came out, followed by Marie. He had a compress over his right eye.

"Can you at least stop your nagging!" he said. "God knows it's unpleasant enough as it is!"

Marie bit her lip and cautiously stroked his arm.

"Poor thing," she said pityingly, as if she were talking to a kindergarten child, "I didn't mean it like that! I merely said that you shouldn't have spoken to him in such a tone of voice."

Now she took his arm in earnest and went on tenderly:

"It's awful the way he hit you! My poor boy! But you know you shouldn't have said that the fishermen were merely local color, and that they couldn't live by fishing under any circumstances!"

He tore himself away and put on a macho face.

"There you go again! You follow me around and nag, nag, nag! But you must try just once to understand that I said that because he answered with such insolence the first time I spoke to him.

Fishermen are children, and they don't understand that they would completely destroy the town if they built a breakwater here. The tourists would disappear, and the fishing is much too poor to provide the town with a living."

"Yes, but it used to support them," said Marie.

"Everything was different then. The sea here is all fished out, it's no longer worth anything. They fished with dynamite for years—can't you see what that means? They killed just about all the small fry."

He suddenly clutched his forehead above his eye.

"Ow," he said, "it really hurts!"

"My poor little boy!" said Marie, kissing him. "I'll take care of it."

She carefully removed the compress over his eye.

"Yecch, it really looks ugly! It's turning black and blue!"

"Are you sure? Then I can't go out anymore either. I can't show myself in public with a black eye. It looks terrible."

She cocked her head and squinted at him as at a painting.

"No," she said slowly, "you look beautiful. Kiss me, Arnold!"

They stood there smooching for a long time.

"Oh," said Marie, "that was nice. You know what? I really think that that black eye becomes you!"

"Yes," I said, "and besides, you got it in a fight for a worthy cause."

"Shut up!" he replied. "Have yourself a gin and vermouth instead. Then you won't talk."

That was all the respect he had for me. Meanwhile Marie replaced the compress.

"There! Now you'll soon be fine again."

"They're actually still fascists, these fishermen. That I wouldn't have believed."

Marie replied:

"Yes, imagine! They're still mad about Mussolini! And Stalin too!"

"I could have told you that," I said into my glass. "But you're much too enlightened and progressive to believe it."

Arnold, harshly:

"They haven't a clue what democracy is!"

Marie said:

"I have to go out and get groceries. But there's vermouth on the table."

I got up, while she poured some into a glass for him and added lemon peel and gin.

"Sit in your chair, love, and take things easy for a bit!"

He sat down, and she caressed him.

"'Bye then. Hope you feel better."

Marie and I went down the stairs together.

She said:

"It was nice of you to come, Anso! But Arnold can't stand to be helped. He simply can't bear to be in anyone's debt. It's his character. Arnold is so manly."

"Yes," I said, "it was mighty manly of him to take offense at me instead of saying thank you."

"None of you understand him."

"Oh yes," I said, "I understand him just fine. He's a bestselling author in French, with socialist leanings. And he can't understand why the Italian workingmen don't prostrate themselves with gratitude. Besides, any old turd can become a bestselling author in French!"

"You are petty and jealous!" she said.

"Yes," I said, "and the next time he gets beat up by a fisherman, I'll let him lie there. In French one gets to be a bestseller just by saying woof! Then one becomes the hope of France!"

Now Marie was really disgusted with me.

"I had no idea you were so mean," she said.

"Ha!" I said, "there are unexpected depths of baseness in me."

"I don't think you like me," she said, taking my hand. "Why do you keep company almost only with the fishermen and—and the natives?"

"I like them," I said.

"Yes, but Anso, they're just using you! You don't understand it yourself, but where foreigners are concerned they don't care about anything but our money."

"No," I said, "they aren't like that with me. They've often helped me, and I've often got fish or fruit or wine from them without being allowed to pay for it."

She looked at me pityingly.

"Don't you understand that you will pay for it another time? Here you have to pay for *everything*! Now Arnold and I have lived here long enough that I'm beginning to know them. Every time they smile at you they secretly add it to the price of something or other. Every smile costs money. They're *playing* Italians by being the way they think the foreigners expect them to be!"

"That type exists too, but the Italians despise them."

"Anso, you're wrong! One day they'll clean you out! I wouldn't be poor here for the world. They'd let both Arnold and me starve to death on the street!"

"Yes," I said, "they would. And quite rightly. That's because you act like an English junior officer's wife in the colonies. You have all the English lower middle class's contempt and fear of what you typically enough call 'the natives'."

Her face became mottled with red and white blotches, and she was breathing rapidly. "Middle class?" she said.

"No," I said, "*lower* middle class."

Instead of getting mad, she looked very unhappy. "What am I doing wrong, then?"

"You could try saying hello to people, for instance."

"God, but I can't just say hello to strangers!"

"And then you could ask after their grandmother, and if their brother in Naples has gotten out again, and if their cousin in America is through with his military service."

"But that's impossible, Anso! That just isn't done!"

"And then you can buy a coffee for the folks who hang out in the bars, and tell them that the government is very bad and is a disgrace to Italy and that you hate it."

"But it's much better than the fascists were?"

"Yes, of course. But that has nothing to do with it. At any rate you must stop being a junior officer's wife going around tight-lipped and looking British. That's out of date now. There's nobody who admires you for it anymore."

"No, England is no longer what it was," she said, and smiled bravely.

"And besides, everybody knows that you aren't married, and that Arnold is no great shakes as a writer, but just writes indecent bestsellers. These fishermen who can't read, they know whole cantos of Dante by heart, and they know that their ancestors were helping build the temple of Neptune there in Paestium at a time when the French were climbing around in trees and the English were walking on all fours and howling at the moon. The only thing which impresses people here is if you've been well brought-up and learned to greet people. That has been good form on this coast for a little over three thousand years."

"God!" said Marie, "I never thought of that!"

"I'm sorry," I said, "but now we must break off this cozy conversation, for I forgot my glasses up at Arnold's, and I don't have another extra pair. See you this afternoon!"

"It was nice chatting with you," she said feebly. "We'll have to continue it some other time."

Then she went on, and I climbed up the stairs again. It had done me good to be nasty to Marie, because the whole time on the terrace I'd been sitting and thinking about The Girl, and how silly I'd made myself look when I met her. Serve them right! I pictured The Girl with her slender, tanned face and her half-blonde, sand-colored hair. She had such a lovely neck, and such a graceful, delicate body. At the same time it had also been a relief to tear down Arnold to Marie, for of course I was jealous of him, writing in French and being reviewed in the whole world press every time he said woof.

Just before I got up to the terrace I heard that he wasn't alone; I peeked over the edge and saw Pamela come cautiously out through the glass door and look around for Marie. I immediately ducked down again.

"Has she gone?" I heard Pamela's voice.

"Yes," replied Arnold's.

"Oh, quick, quick, while we're alone, then!"

There was a long pause, but with some deep breathing, and then Arnold spoke, heavily and with effort:

"I had no idea that Marie had such lovely friends! It's a shame we didn't meet earlier."

Another pregnant silence followed, and it was great fun to stand on the stairs. Then Pamela whispered hoarsely:

"I had to take this trip first! Imagine, if I hadn't come we might never have met. You're a beautiful man, Arnold! Oh, you're wonderful, my little honeybunch! I admired you so on the beach this morning. He looked terrible; he was spurting fire!"

Arnold:

"But still he's your beloved from this morning; you did say for all to hear that he was the handsomest man in Bellapalma. Now what the hell is his name?"

Pamela:

"Tomaso. He's a fisherman. Is he terribly strong, then?"

"He hit hard enough, at any rate."

"I'll never speak to him again. I admired you so terribly when you spoke to him like that. I don't know how you dared. You were so brave!"

Arnold's voice:

"You think so?"

As I stood there listening to all this, I was thinking all the while about The Girl, and at the same time wishing I could hit on something nasty to say about Arnold. That's doubtless why I hadn't noticed that Georg had come up the stairs and was now standing silently behind me. I knew him by the winy smell. He was even more red-faced than usual, and looked uncommonly hale and sunburned.

"So you're spying!" I said.

"Be my guest," he said. "You mustn't deny yourself anything!"

"Be nice and don't tell them!" I begged.

From above we heard Pamela's voice:

"You were splendid, you were!"

Georg smiled.

"You must admit that it's delightful to listen to?" I said. But Georg didn't reply, he just walked quietly past me and soundlessly up onto the terrace. I followed him halfway, so that I was standing with my upper body above the edge of the terrace, and at the same time was hidden behind him.

"Excuse me!" said Georg, but they didn't hear, they were too busy kissing. He repeated:

"Excuse me!!"

Pamela jumped, and flashed at him:

"Oh, God!" she cried, "You're spying, too!"

"Yes," said Georg, "I never miss a chance to sneak up on people if I get one. But you must forgive me for disturbing the harmonious relations between man and wife. How many wives do you have, Arnold? And how's your eye, my poor friend? I don't suppose you have the kind of flesh that heals very fast."

"Shut up!" said Arnold. "Did you come just to torment me?"

"No, I have some big news. But first I must taste your excellent vermouth. May I?"

"What's the news?"

"Real news! Things are happening now in Bellapalma, events and things, you know, which have never happened before. Skaal, Arnold! And skaal, dear lady! And skaal to the people!"

I came all the way up and stuck my glasses in my pocket. Now I was willing to do anything in the world to avoid thinking of The Girl, but I couldn't figure out what.

"Did you come from the beach?" said Arnold to Georg.

"Yes, they're still at it. That is, they're just beginning! It's getting to be a real revolt now. The fishermen won't give in, and they're gathering at Alexi's tonight to continue the meeting. The whole town is standing on its head. You can hardly get a cup of coffee."

"It must be awful for you to be without coffee!" said Arnold venemously.

Georg mixed himself another drink.

"But that's terrible!" said Pamela. "All the decent people ought to leave, then they can see how they like it. They'll destroy the whole town now!"

"It's their town," said Georg.

"It's like a bad dream," said Arnold, looking pained. "Are they communists or fascists?"

"You could say they've skimmed the cream off both movements," said Georg. "They're sort of fasci-communists, but without the typical mass movement's hatred of the intellectuals."

"How disgusting," said Pamela. "I'd never dream of becoming a communist! You can see right there that they aren't Americans."

"Mussolini and the communists are the only ones who've taken an interest in the small fishermen's welfare," said Georg, "and therefore they love them. The older ones can't read."

"But the social democrats!" cried Arnold. "Don't they know what the social democrats are doing for them?"

"In this country it's the upper classes who are social democrats. They live on the Riviera."

"God!" said Arnold. He clutched his head, and it was clear that his eye was hurting. I smiled, for I'd never really liked him very much.

Georg was now mixing himself a third drink. "As an old socialist, Arnold, you should be on the rebels' side."

Arnold said:

"I'm thinking of what's best for them."

"You disagreed with them this morning!"

"For their own good, yes! The tourists are much more important for the town than the lousy fishing can ever be. Economically it's much more important."

"Man does not live by tourists alone," replied Georg.

"Nonsense!" said Arnold. "Here they live on tourists. On tourists and nothing but. They're all waiters, even the fishermen in reality. Their mission in life is to rent out their boats in the tourist season, while they themselves sit on the beach and get their pictures taken. They're all waiters!"

Now Pamela too made known her estimable opinion:

"It's like that everywhere here. They live by tourists alone."

"Even fishermen have souls," Georg persisted doggedly. "All right, most of them are happy illiterates, Arnold, but they do have *soul*, even if they have to get along without reading your distinguished books!"

"Soul!" snorted Arnold. "What kind of religious claptrap is that? You're a German, Georg, and ergo a metaphysician. And soul has nothing to do with it. Besides, you're drunk. How many have you had today?"

"Not so very many, I don't think," said Georg pensively, while he attempted to count on his fingers.

Arnold said:

"And what's going on in the town now?"

"A common ordinary riot. The mayor has called in the police to help this evening, and he's coming himself to the meeting at Alexi's to read the riot act and talk them around."

"Who's leading them?" said Pamela.

"It's Tomaso, whom you chatted so cozily with at the Sunshine this morning, and whom Arnold struck up such a warm friendship with on the beach a while later."

"Some leader!" said Arnold.

"Yes," said Georg, "he's as if born to put ideas into action. He's illiterate and a natural political leader type. He's demanding that work on the tourist houses be stopped immediately, and that they start building the breakwater instead. It will take about two months to build the harbor if they all keep at it."

"They're courting their own ruin!" said Arnold.

"No," said Georg very seriously, "they want to regain their dignity as seamen and as fishermen. That's really the whole issue. Without knowing it, and without having the wherewithal to understand it, you in fact hit the nail on the head, or rather the fisherman in the solar plexus, by what you said this morning on the beach."

"Namely?"

"Namely that both they and their boats are just window dressing which has to be there to make the tourists feel that they're living in a fishing village. They're *decoration*, you said; and they'll have to get used to being that for the sake of the tourist industry which supports everybody."

"So?"

"Well, they don't want to do that anymore. You yourself helped to open their eyes. They have their pride, and sometimes they put it even above socioeconomic considerations."

"Was that what you meant by saying that they had souls?" said Pamela.

"Yes, pretty much."

There was a brief silence, then Georg turned and pointed at me:

"By the way," he said, "I can also inform you that our little friend Hans was on the stairs eavesdropping before I came. I found him standing there listening to your whole amorous interlude."

"What!" said both of them at once.

"You scoundrel!" I said, "so you're telling tales!"

All three stood there staring at me, and I could feel myself getting red in the face. For quite a long time nobody said anything.

I tried to get a conversation going.

"It's frightfully tiresome with this atomic bomb," I said. "It's downright disgusting that they've started these tests."

Georg looked gravely at me:

"Yes, and then completely behind your back!"

A sobbing girl came onto the terrace. I had seen her before in Bellapalma; she is in her late twenties, pretty, somewhat chubby, and has long, very light hair. There is a steady supply of such girls here. Now her face was red and streaming as she looked around. It was clear that she was searching for someone.

"Kari!" said Georg. "What are you doing here?"

"Oh, thank God you're here, Georg! Something terrible has happened. Oh, something just awful!"

Suddenly she broke down completely, and was only kept on her feet by Arnold and Pamela supporting her between them. She was weeping loudly, and couldn't speak. I wondered if I should take the opportunity to disappear, but I was too curious to leave.

"This is Kari." Georg introduced her guardedly. "She's from Copenhagen or Stockholm or one of those places. She has lived here for four or five years. I met her last winter. So tell us about it, Kari! Take it easy, my friend!"

Some hoarse sounds came out:

"Oh, oh Lord! This is the most awful experience of my life!"

Her voice dissolved into sobs again. She shook and wept convulsively, while they tried to calm her with stroking.

"Whatever happened, it must have been something uncommonly dreadful," said Georg. "She's usually a very tranquil girl, I've never seen her like this before. Usually she's placid, like everybody from Scandinavia."

"Scandinavia?" said Pamela. "Where's that? Is it something to do with the Baltic, or—or maybe Balkan is what it's called?"

"Nonsense!" said Arnold. "It's a town in Sweden. She's Swedish, surely you can see that! A completely natural blonde."

"And I'm not natural, I suppose?" said Pamela.

"Yes," said Arnold, "but you're not blonde."

Now a series of wild shrieks came from Kari.

"But what is it then?" asked Pamela. "Is it something which concerns us all?"

"Yes, yes, everybody! It's finished! It's over! Oh, oh!"

"It must be something very serious," said Georg anxiously. "Probably she's witnessed someone being stabbed, or some such. It looks as if she's had a shock."

Pamela led her over to a chair and sat her down in it.

"Sit down now, poor thing! You need a little drink!"

She made her a dry martini.

"Here!"

Arnold looked uncomfortably at Georg.

"So it wasn't a joke, what you said about the stabbing this morning?"

Georg grew animated:

"A joke, no! I tell you it's an absolute national scourge here! Somebody's always getting stabbed. They're really good at it, and they don't do it the way we think at all. They don't hold the knife by the handle the way we do."

He picked up a fruit knife from the table to illustrate what he was trying to explain, and held it so that the end of the haft rested against the inside of his palm while the pinched-together fingers supported the knife.

"That's how they hold it," he explained, "the way we hold a walking stick, the kind without a curved handle. That way they keep their hand from slipping down over the blade when they hit home. And they can stab with much more force. Like this!"

He lunged at Arnold with the fruit knife. Arnold recoiled, curling his upper lip in a grimace of repugnance.

"What the hell!" said he. "That's disgusting."

"Oh," cried Kari, "this is the worst, most horrible experience of my life! Are you here, Georg? Come hold my hand!"

"Poor little girl," he said, taking her gently by the hand. "Tell me now, Kari. Was it horrible?"

She sobbed in hollow, protracted sobs:

"Dreadful, oh, dreadful!"

"Say what it is, Kari! Say it, my friend!"

"You can see the letter," she wailed, and began rooting in her purse. She was blinded by tears, and didn't find it at once.

"The letter?" said Georg. "It isn't the riot?"

"Look here! Oh! Boo-hoo! Hoo! See for yourself!"

He took the letter, unfolded it, and became absorbed in it.

"Good grief!" he said after a while. "That's extraordinary!"

Pamela and Arnold cried in one breath:

"What is it? Tell us, then!"

He didn't hear, but stared wordlessly at Kari, who continued to weep and wail:

"Didn't I say so?" she blubbered. "It's the worst thing that's ever happened to me!"

"Just a month left!" said Georg, stunned.

Pamela grabbed him and shook him as if she wanted to call him back to life, but he let her shake away without noticing. His head wobbled under Pamela's strong hands.

"Georg!" I said harshly, "the American people want to talk to you!"

"Good God, Kari!" he said softly. "This concerns us all!"

She merely stared at him.

"What is it?" said Pamela. "Say it! Say it!"

Georg woke up and turned to her.

"What did you say?" he said.

"Tell us what happened! What is this experience of Kari's?"

"Oh," said Georg, "she's being expelled."

"She what?" asked Pamela.

"What is she expelled from?" Arnold chimed in.

"She's being expelled from Bellapalma. They've given her a month's notice. In other words, she won't get her residence permit renewed."

"Can you be expelled from here?" said Arnold, taken aback.

"And what are the grounds?" asked Pamela. "What has she done?"

George looked inquiringly at Kari, who nodded to him.

"Hm," he said, "um. She is being expelled because of her, um, behavior."

Pamela and Arnold cried both at once:

"What?! Is it true?"

Kari nodded and sobbed:

"Oh God, yes! It's in the letter—but it isn't true! I haven't done anything but what everybody else does here!"

Then she raised her head and shrieked at the top of her lungs:

"They're completely natural things!"

All the men jumped at the violent outburst.

"How's that, Georg?" said Pamela, undisturbed. "It sounds so terribly wrong!"

"I'm afraid she has been a mite careless of her reputation, poor thing," said Arnold thoughtfully.

Kari had filled her lungs with new air.

"I've never done anything but what everybody does here! I—oh! I can't live anywhere but in Bellapalma!"

"Can't she find a place in one of the neighboring towns and settle there for a while?" said Pamela.

Georg looked again at the letter.

"That won't work. She's being expelled from the whole country."

Arnold took charge of the discussion:

"That's probably true," he said. "I have a friend who's been banished from five European countries. From France, Italy, Portugal, Switzerland, and…no, I don't remember the fifth."

"And what's the reason for it?" said Pamela.

"In his case it's two things. Drunkenness as with Georg, and… and…indecent behavior as with Miss Kari. But that was more than a year ago, and today he's been expelled from even more places."

"Oh God!" said Pamela. "He's like a refugee, poor man! Traveling from country to country, homeless in the world!"

"That's quite common now." Arnold went on. "You can call it a postwar phenomenon."

"Couldn't he visit the Faroe Islands?" I said, to show that I was sympathetic. "They're supposed to have rather free social conventions."

"Yes," said Georg, "but that's just the trouble, he's from the Faroe Islands."

We all felt that things looked dark for him, but in the meantime Kari had drawn a breath. If you can imagine an elephant in labor, you'll get a relatively correct impression of her intonation:

"Oh, oh, oh!…Now I have to go home to Oslo! Oh—!"

She burst into wild sobs, and we became utterly still.

"To what?" said Pamela. "What did she say?"

"Ask her!" said Arnold to Georg.

"Kari! Where must you go from here, Kari?"

"To O—ah, ha, ha,—Os—! Oslo! I'll go mad!"

Georg straightened up, for he had bent down to understand her better.

"It sounds as if she's saying Oslo."

We looked at each other.

"Yes, that's what she said," opined Arnold.

"Where's that?" said Pamela.

"It's in Finland," I said. "Northern Finland."

"Oh, Lord!" groaned Pamela.

Almost a minute passed in silence.

"Have any of you seen Martin?" asked Georg.

"He hasn't been here," said Pamela.

"I've been looking for him for hours, and it's an utter madhouse in town. Devil take him! Do you want to come to the Sunshine? He may be on the Piazza."

Kari had stopped crying now, and sat eating Arnold with her eyes.

"God, yes! Let's go then!" cried Pamela. "I must see what's happening in the town!"

"I can't show myself outside with this eye," said Arnold. "I'll stay home. But buy a pair of sunglasses, Pamela, so I can wear them this afternoon."

"I'll do that."

"Can I please stay here for a bit? Only a little while? I'm so unhappy."

This Kari addressed to Arnold, and began crying again.

"You're welcome to stay here and relax a little," he replied tenderly. "I can understand that it must be terrible. And then… Os…what was it called, Kari?"

"Oslo," she replied, and cast down her eyes.

"Hope you feel better, Arnold," said Georg. "And try to think about something else, Kari."

So the three of us went off, leaving them alone with their wounds. I tried to get Georg and Pamela to go on ahead, but it didn't work; he stuck to my side, and Pamela went first. I slowed down to get rid of him, but he kept the same easy pace as I. Pamela was walking faster than we were, and when we turned from the stairs into the street, she was a long way ahead.

"You seem so edgy," said Georg. "Is something the matter, Hans?"

"No," I said bitterly. We walked a little further. Then I stopped.

"Georg," I said, "I'm sorry, but I have to leave you now. I forgot my glasses up on the terrace."

"No," said he, "I saw you stick them in your pocket."

"Georg," I said pleadingly, "I want to so dreadfully!"

He turned and stood still.

"Seriously, Anso! I think this is a rather odd trait of yours."

"Will you promise not to say anything this time?"

"No," he said.

"I know a lot about you, Georg, which I've never told anybody!"

"Well, you can just tell it, then!"

"Georg! Now he's showing her the apartment!"

"Do as you like," he said, and went on.

I followed after him, but got mad and walked hurriedly past him and down the street.

"Anso! Don't sulk, then!"

I didn't hear him, he was air to me, and I swung up to the left to be quit of him. He didn't follow.

Then I caught sight of Matteo, and got furious. He saw me too, ducked his head, and tried to disappear into a little side street.

"Matteo!" I shouted, "Don't run away! I've seen you!"

He turned around and came slowly over to me. He looked embarrassed.

"You're the worst boy in Bellapalma," I said. "Yes, you are!"

"Very dearest, buonissimo *professore*…"

"Don't you '*professore*' me! You're a bandit and a bad person. Why am I paying you four thousand a month, you lazy good-for-nothing?"

"To look after you, *professore*."

"And what did you do yesterday? Did you maybe look after me? You blasted Neapolitan, you Sicilian!"

"*Reverendissimo professore*, my grandmother was very sick! Oh, she was awful terrible sick, and she was coughing!"

"And what about me?" I yelled. "Look here!" And I rolled up my left pantleg and showed him the blue and yellow marks and the two abrasions.

"*Carissimo professore*! That is just terrible!"

"Yes," I said, "it is *veramente* terrible. And who do I have to thank for it?"

He hung his head and didn't dare look at me.

"All right," I said, "and then the car. Had you maybe removed the spark plug cables the way I taught you to do when I'm under the influence?"

"No, *professore*, greatest of all *professori*! My grandmother. . . ."

"I don't want to hear another word about your wretched, reprehensible grandmother! Does she maybe pay you four thousand? I went to my car last night, and I would have started it if I hadn't by pure chance forgotten the keys. I would have driven up the road, and might have plunged over the cliff, and then I wouldn't be here today. And it would have been your fault."

"Dreadful, *professore*! *Terribilissimo*!"

"And what are you supposed to do if I fall asleep on the street?"

"Sit beside you and keep watch, best of all *professori*."

"Couldn't I maybe have fallen asleep yesterday?"

"Yes, *professore*, you very well might have."

"Matteo, am I served by a guard like you?"

"Very dearest, most generous *professore*!"

"Matteo, I could hit you!"

"*Grandissimo professore*, can't you beat me a little instead of being so stern with me?"

"I never hit anyone younger than me; they're stronger."

"I'll mend my ways, *professore*!"

"Maybe I'll never be under the influence again," I said, "and then I won't need you. This morning I was very close to deciding never to drink wine again, for I don't want people to think I'm a drunk."

"*Professore...*!"

"No," I said, "you're fired. It's finished between us. I'll hire another minder."

His shoulders began to shake. "Perhaps I can be a minder for *signore* Georg?"

"No," I said more gently, "it's out of the question. He is a very cold and evil person. He would treat you badly."

Matteo's mouth quivered, and his long eyelashes grew wet. My heart melted.

"Well, I'll see if I can keep you all the same, Matteo. On probation."

He brightened.

"*Professore*, can I have a hundred lire today?"

I gave him a coin and he thanked me politely. Then he went bounding down the side street, jumped over ten feet of stairs and was gone. Far down on the beach I heard his voice:

"Ragazzi! Ragazzi! Oh—oh—oh—!"

Matteo was happy again.

Then I went on, and when I passed Giovanni's grocery I saw that he had strawberries. It was early in the year, but they didn't impress me. And they didn't look clean or appetizing either. It was only when I came to Emanuele's old, black cellar of a shop that I stood still. For he too had strawberries. And what strawberries! They were large, deep red, and moist. I'd practically never seen strawberries like that. And they were clean. They were spotlessly clean. Never in all my misspent life have I seen such clean strawberries! There wasn't a grain of stand on them. I bent over the display of boxes and looked closely at the berries under the cellophane.

Nowhere do they take hygiene so seriously as in Italy—once they make up their minds to do so. It probably has to do with the fact that the concept "hygiene" still has novelty's power to excite, and they wash and rinse everything with the greatest fanaticism. Naturally the strawberries would be expensive, but still I felt a great yen for them, and I went into the half-dark shop.

It was Emanuele's grandchild, the forty-year-old Mallerina, who stood behind the counter.

"*Buon giorno*! Most excellent *signorina*! You have extremely delicious strawberries!"

"Yes," she said shyly, "we've sold several baskets already." And she smiled with satisfaction. "We've sold far more than Giovanni, who also has strawberries, and that's because ours are as clean as the stars in the sky."

"I'll take a basket," I said, and she began wrapping them up.

"We've come a long way now," said Mallarina, "with progress and culture, *professore*. We're extremely intelligent in Italy."

"How are things with Emanuele?" I said. "Does he still have his awful cough?"

"Oh yes," she said. "Grandfather is still poorly, a very frail old man. But he's sitting there in the back room working. Won't you say hello to him, *professore*?"

I went down a few more steps and into the musty tomb of a back room, where old Emanuele lived. He turned toward me and smiled his good, toothless smile.

"God bless you, *professore*, for visiting an exceedingly old and feeble man!"

"You aren't feeble, *reverendissimo* Emanuele. You are a man of iron. Your generation is stronger than mine."

"Thanks to Mary's exceeding grace," he said, "I can still work, and I have strong eyes with good sight."

And he turned toward the light from the small, vine-covered window, and continued cleaning the strawberries. He took every single berry by the stem, blew on it, and held it up to the light. Then he licked it carefully with his large, pink tongue, looked at it again, and then held it up to me. There wasn't a grain of sand left on the berry. Thereupon he laid it in the box with the finished ones.

"*Buonissimo* Emanuele," I said, "bless your work!"

"*Buon appetito*, professore, and a good rest afterwards!"

I took the package on the counter, paid and went out. And I headed for Alexi's to get some dinner. I was hungry.

As I rounded the corner, I bumped into Marie, who was still doing her shopping. I was sad and lonely.

"Hi, Marie, come along up to Alexi's!"

"That's very kind of you, Anso! But I've eaten."

"Just come along and keep me company for a little," I pled.

"I'm really sorry, but I don't have time. I have a lot of shopping to do."

"Can't you just sit up there for a little while? Just while I'm waiting for my food?"

"It's impossible, Anso."

"Marie?"

"Yes?"

"There's something I have to say to you."

"What's that?"

"I'm sorry I was unpleasant to you a while ago."

"No, but Anso! It was just good that you said it!"

"Yes, but I said it in such a nasty way."

"Yes, that's true. I was really humiliated by it."

"So I bought you some strawberries. Please take them if you'd like them!"

Her face lit up and she smiled.

"Are they really strawberries? How sweet of you!" She gave me a kiss on the cheek.

"They're the first of the year," I said, feeling a little proud.

"You're sweet," she said. "That's really touching!"

"You might give Arnold some, too!" I said.

Then she left, and I climbed to the second floor at Alexi's and sat down at a table. I was the only one in the whole dining room, and I felt terribly down and dejected. I was feeling quite ashamed that I had eavesdropped on Arnold and Pamela. Carola came up with the menu, and I took off my glasses and immersed myself in it. She set the wine carafe on the table and went down again. Looking at the menu made me feel better because I was going to eat, and because I was hungry. I sat thus for a good while, mentally tasting each dish and asking myself if I wanted it. In fact I patted myself on the shoulder and was nice to myself. Someone came in and sat at the side table, but I calmly went on reading the menu. Only after a little while did I put on my glasses and raise my head to see who had come in.

It was The Girl.

THREE

Yes, it was The Girl sitting there.

I checked to make sure that I was wearing my glasses and was really seeing right, but it was her. She sat looking at me, a smile on her thin, young face. My heart flipped like a big mountain trout after a fly, and I felt the pulse all the way out in my wrists and fingers. My mouth grew dry, and my throat knotted up so that I could neither smile nor say hello. It came out as a grimace this time too, and I couldn't manage a sound. And I felt my face getting red as a beet. Finally I tried to hide my feet under my chair because they're so terribly big. But a blush went through her this time too, I noticed that—I still had that many of my wits about me.

I took off my glasses again so I wouldn't have to look at her, and my hands were shaking so much that I almost didn't manage. Reaching for the wine carafe to fill my glass, I knocked it over and spilled wine on the table. I downed two glasses one after another.

It helped, and I calmed down. After a while I looked at her without my glasses, making her seem misty and rather faraway. Then I saw only the colors of her, and that was easier. Her face and hair were a pale wisp of fog, and I couldn't see if she was looking at me. Then I polished off the carafe; now my mood changed completely, so that the cramp in my throat knotted up again.

I put on my glasses and stared at her. She didn't notice, but sat looking for something which had fallen on the floor. On the table in front of her lay a sketch pad.

She got out of her chair and went down on all fours to search better, and now I got into the act. I went over and got down on my hands and knees a ways off from her. Then I searched eagerly for a while, crawling around the table. Presently we came face to face on the floor.

"*Buon giorno!*" I said pleasantly.

"*Salve!*" said she, "*sempre avanti!*"

"What!" I said. "Where did you learn to greet people like that?"

"From Cesare," she replied. "He has told me lots about you."

"It's all lies!" I answered.

"Cesare never lies!"

Pause.

"It's so nice to have a reason to lie on the floor," I said, and lay down flat on my stomach.

"Mm," she said, "this is lovely."

"What are we looking for?"

"My eraser."

We looked for a while longer.

"How did you get to know Cesare?"

"I have secret powers," she said.

"Cesare is very choosy about the company he keeps. It speaks in your favor that he wants to associate with you."

Then I found the eraser.

"Here you are."

She rose to her knees:

"Many thanks! But there's something I have to tell you!"

"Yes?"

"I dropped it on the floor on purpose. So that I could make your acquaintance."

"That was nice of you," I said. "Otherwise, nothing would have happened."

"I didn't see any other way."

I got to my feet, and she stood up too.

"We could eat at the same table," I said. "Then we'd only dirty one tablecloth. I've already messed up mine, so it's best that we sit at my table."

She took her things and moved them over.

"This is terrible," she said. "You've already drunk up the whole carafe. There's not a drop left. And it was half a liter."

"Without that," said I, "even your ploy with the eraser wouldn't have helped."

"How are you going to get along when you go out into the world?"

She looked at me with concern.

"Everybody says that."

"Is it true that you have Matteo as a minder?" she said.

"Yes. But he's a miserable watchman. He doesn't do me much good. If his most dreadful grandmother hadn't been so sick, I would have sacked him."

"We might as well be friends," she said.

"Yes, since you ask!" I replied.

She curled up in her chair and peered at me.

"Anso," she said, "I've long wanted so terribly much to get to know you!"

"Hm," I said, and picked up the carafe to see if there wasn't something left in it after all.

"This morning," she went on, "I almost thought you were going to speak to me, but you were too stuck up to notice me."

"Stuck up?"

"Well, embarrassed, then! But you know you don't ever need to be embarrassed in front of me, because I know all about you."

"How's that?"

"Because I've been spying on you for five weeks."

"I don't like nosy-parkers," I said.

"And then I know Tomaso and Matteo and Cesare," she went on. "And so I know that you aren't crazy, just *molto nervoso!*"

"Does he really go around saying that?"

"No, I had to pry it out of him."

"I don't understand what you want with me," I said. "I'm not handsome, I'm not fun, I'm not rich, and I'm not famous. I'm not even young and slender."

"You're nice!" said she. "Because Tomaso said so."

"No," I said, "I'm really extremely naughty. Once I gave a lady some strawberries an old man had licked. But of course that was a long time ago."

"I know that it was the English lady you gave the strawberries to."

"No," I said, "now you're lying! Because it's not true and there's nobody who saw it."

Now I went downstairs and said to Carola that we would have squid and mussels and more white wine. It was chock full on the ground floor, and the atmosphere was noisy and threatening. Tension lay in the air, and it was evident that something was going to happen any minute.

When I came up again The Girl was sitting motionless at the table, as if in thought. She had shaken her head so that her hair hung down in her face. She looked naughty and unruly.

I sat down.

"Girl!" I said, "have you done something you shouldn't?"

"Yes," she said, "I'm in bad trouble."

"Have you been stealing?" I said.

"Worse."

"What if we ran away to Africa?" I suggested. "I've also done a lot of wrong things. But they aren't all discovered yet. And if we steal a motorboat we can get across in a couple of days. The police are really wretched over there."

"No," she said, "that will have to wait for another time, because I have to leave when we've eaten."

"That's not true."

"Yes, I have to leave town."

"Then I'll drink myself to death. I'll sink quick as lighting into wild and satanic drunkenness and die the death."

"I must," she said.

"I've had an unhappy childhood," I said, "a really hard and grey time."

"I'll be back."

"When?"

"Don't know."

"Can't we agree on a time?"

"No. I'll be back in a few days, and then I'll find you."

Now Carola came up with the wine and laid the table for us. Soon we were sitting there eating.

"This wasn't part of the plan," she said.

"What?"

"That I should get a dinner off you."

"No," I said, "you should be ashamed. Going around cadging dinners from people! And then leaving town afterwards!"

She peered at me again, curling up in her chair.

"When I get back," she said, "then I want to take a siesta with you too!"

When we'd finished eating we went out onto the street from the second floor, and it was hot and oppressive outside, much warmer than inside the trattoria where there was shade and a draft. In the street a sultry, moist wind was blowing.

"Is it scirocco or mezzogiorno?" she asked.

"Scirocco," I said. "It's famous for attacking the nerves—if one has any."

We went a ways up the street together. The town was a hornet's nest, murmuring and buzzing, and it wasn't easy to make headway. She stopped and gave me her hand.

"Goodbye, Anso! It was fun."

I mumbled something and looked at her.

"I really am coming back," she said, "but I don't know when."

She sprang up a side staircase and was gone. I went on alone.

Then someone called to me higher up the street, and I looked up. A little, well-dressed gentleman came running down.

"*Professore, professore!*" It was Strozzi, the chief of the Tourist Bureau.

"Dearest of all tourist chiefs!"

He reached me, bowed, greeted me, apologized and wriggled.

"*Carissimo professore!* There are dreadful things afoot in Bellapalma!"

"Yes, *signor* tourist chief; I think it may get more serious than people think."

"*Professore*, may I be permitted to make a request of you?"

"Of course, *signor* Strozzi, but I'm not a man who can answer prayers. Unless they are of a very simple nature."

"Because of the situation in the town we're holding a meeting a little later today at *signor* Lippi's excellent hotel. That is: we, the town fathers who bear responsibility for the common weal, we're gathering to discuss the situation over a simple dinner. We have to find a solution. It will be the police chief, the mayor, *signore* Lippi and myself. *Monsignor* Leone has also promised to attend."

"Best of all tourist chiefs, I can't find praise enough for whoever among these gentleman has taken the initiative to call such a meeting. I believe it can save the town."

He blushed with pride:

"Now it is our humble plea, *professore*, that you too will place your intelligence and experience of the world at our disposal by taking part in the meeting?"

"Highly excellent tourist chief, my intelligence is extremely low; it is a most wretched intelligence."

"*Carissimo e grandissimo professore*! Your experience and reading are enormous, and we regard the battle as lost if you cannot overcome your modesty and join us."

"Excellent tourist chief, what you say about my experience may be correct, and it is also true that I've read more than most people. But still I am very sentimental, and my imagination is uncommonly great, but my reason has always been very weakly developed. My presence will retard the negotiations rather than furthering them."

"*Professore*, may we expect you at three o'clock?"

"*Signor* tourist chief, you do me a great honor."

He nodded and went back up the street.

Up on the Piazza del Sole it was almost impossible to get through, and everyone was excited. I didn't know how soon the tension would reach the flash point, and whether I would be late for the meeting of the town fathers. I only knew that I still had a few minutes, and I sat down in front of the Sunshine, behind the door on the outside, so that I could sit quite alone and unnoticed for a while. The workmen with their baskets of rocks were continually crossing the square.

Marie glided past me and into the bar to Mario.

"Oh, Mario! Can you keep a secret?"

"It's only rarely that I find out anything, *signora*, but then I'm silent as the grave."

"That fisherman who was here today, what was his name?"

"Tomaso."

"Well, I simply must make his acquaintance! I'm so afraid that something will happen between him and Mr. Arnold. And so I thought you could arrange it?—No, please, Mario! Keep the change!"

"Oh, thank you, many thanks, *signora*!"

"Can you manage it?"

"Yes, *signora*, he's coming here this afternoon, and then I'll arrange a time with him."

"You're so sweet, Mario!"

Now Pamela came fluttering by me and into the bar. She would have seen me if she hadn't first spotted Marie through the big window. When she saw her, her skin darkened.

"God, how restless they are today!" she cried. "I think people have gone completely crazy. You can't even get through the streets! Is it the fishermen who are making all this commotion?"

Mario: "Yes, I don't understand it. It's never been like this in Bellapalma before. They're destroying the whole town. And they'll use force, they say, if it becomes necessary. But now *signore* Lippi and the mayor and the police chief are going to have a meeting and consider what they should do. —But I hear that Mr. Arnold was injured on the beach. Not seriously, I hope?"

Marie and Pamela, loudly and eagerly in unison:

"Oh, no! It's not worth mentioning!"

"I have to go do some shopping," said Marie. "Are you staying, Pamela?"

"Yes, for a while. So long!"

"Au revoir, *signora*!"

Marie glided out again, with downcast eyes.

Pamela's voice:

"Can you keep a secret, Mario?"

"It isn't often that people tell me anything, signora, but then I keep my mouth shut."

"That fisherman who was here this morning, what was his name?"

"Tomaso."

"Yes, that's it! I simply must speak with him, Mario! No, no! Just keep the change!"

"Thank you very much, *signora*!"

"Because I'm so afraid that something serious may happen between him and Mr. Arnold. It could be worse next time!"

"That would be dreadful, *signora*! Just terrible!"

"Yes, terrible! Do you think you can arrange for me to meet him? But nobody must know about it!"

"Nothing is easier, *signora*!"

"Are you sure?"

"I'll be talking with him in a while, and if you come here a little later, then I can tell you where you can meet him."

"Thanks, Mario!"

Georg came over the square, visibly refreshed and unsteady on his feet. He looked bad under the winy color:

"'Lo, Ganymede! Vermouth and gin! 'Lo, Pamela!"

"Good afternoon, *signore*!"

"Have any of you seen Martin? I've been searching for that disgusting boy all day. There isn't a bar in Bellapalma where I haven't looked for him!"

"Nobody tells me anything, *signore*, not a thing in the world!"

Two workmen crossed the piazza meekly and quietly, barefoot, straining under their baskets. They disappeared on the other side, but only for a moment. There were a couple of loud shrieks, then they backed into the square again and stood there. After them came Tomaso and a lot of other fishermen with menacing expressions and clenched fists. One was a tall, red-haired fellow who bore the name Timberio, and whom I had often seen on the beach.

"Put down those baskets!" yelled Tomaso to the workmen: "Put them down!"

Timberio went swiftly past the workmen and stationed himself behind them. He pointed at the ground.

"Put them down!"

"We're not allowed to stop work," said one of the workmen doubtfully. "We must carry them all the way down to the beach!"

Tomaso bared his teeth and pointed downwards with one hand while he gestured in the air with the other.

"Here we're the ones who decide! Put them down! The tourist cabins will stay the way they are. All work on them is canceled. Put down your baskets! As of now plutocracy is finished!"

The workmen crowded together, but stood their ground. Timberio grabbed one of them by the shirt and raised his huge fist: "Let go of the capitalist's highly loathsome baskets! Or else!"

More fishermen accosted them, shouting loudly. Now the baskets sank to the ground, the workers standing bewildered beside them. Tomaso yelled in a powerful voice:

"The ungodly construction is finished now! *Basta*! Not another basket! Down with the tourist houses! *Basta, basta*!"

He looked fearsome, gnashing his teeth, his dark eyes narrowed. Still more workers arrived with baskets on their necks and were stopped by the fishermen, who surrounded them shrieking.

"Slaves!" snarled Tomaso.

"Lackeys of Big Capital!" roared Timberio.

The lackeys drew together and looked unhappy with big brown eyes.

"We won't get paid if we don't work," said one of them meekly.

"You are a bad and evil person!" Tomaso told him.

"Yes, but what shall we do if we don't get paid?"

There were others who chimed in, and some of the fishermen began to look uneasily at Tomaso.

"Ha!" said he, looking around searchingly, "as if we haven't thought of that!" He stood up straight, his eyes sparkling. "Timberio and I are like mother and father to you! We've thought of everything! Haven't we, Timberio?"

"Huh?" said Timberio.

"You are evil people who don't want to understand that tomorrow the work begins on the breakwater, and then you'll have work again. You'll work for us, of course. If you are diligent."

"Yes," said Timberio, "if you'll work hard."

"Oh, we will!"

"As if we aren't just like parents to you!" said Tomaso. "You bad men!"

"Where are you getting the money from?" said one of the workmen.

"You think we haven't thought about money?" said Tomaso, as a brooding expression came over his face. "I've said that I'm like a father to you! What kind of father would I be if I hadn't thought about the money you're going to get? Oh, a most wretched father!"

"Very best Tomaso, what money are you thinking of?" asked Timberio.

"The town treasury!" said Tomaso. "The town will pay for the breakwater. Now it's us poor little lice, us fishermen who make the decisions. Hasn't Bellapalma always been a fishing town, and isn't it extremely natural that the fishermen should make the decisions here?! It's our ancestors who built up this most idiotic town, it is our town! You maybe think it's right for the fishermen to be mocked and despised in their own town?"

Now there arose a great, a mighty cry:

"No! It's our town!"

"Should the lousy waiters maybe run things in a fishing town?" he went on.

"No, no! It's our town!"

"Are fishermen maybe not also human beings to God?" he cried. "Haven't we braved the storm and brought both mussels and squid up from the sea's highly dreadful deep? O Madonna, is this a life to live? When honest fishermen are looked upon as dead cats! Come, signori fishermen, let's go build a harbor right now!"

The enthusiasm was frenetic.

Tomaso drove it further, fanned it, poured oil on the flames.

"Ha!" he shouted. "We're just miserable fishermen! We must be paltry little shrimp! Like extremely small sand fleas! Ha, ha! I have to laugh when I think of us! We're almost invisible without glasses! The waiters have to put specs on to see us! O Madonna, will our humiliation never end?"

Roar, storm, hurricane. The mass movement was set in motion.

"We're coming with you!" shouted a workman.

It caught fire, crackled, exploded. The piazza was a churning sea, the people driven back and forth by the stormy winds and the waves. Whee!

Then came the still, soundless moment where the storm caught its breath. And in the midst of this deathly silence a voice sounded:

"You read as well as a pig, Tomaso! And you want to make a revolution!"

The voice belonged to a very large waiter in a white jacket. Behind him a number of waiters had gathered, all in their uniforms. But Tomaso had no dearth of arguments.

"O Madonna!" he said, "What a thoroughly evil and bad waiter you are! Stick to your plates, you most wretched of all lickspittles!"

His face had turned black and sick with fury, but the big waiter didn't give in.

"You miserable fishermen can't even feed yourselves with your squid! And then the whole town is supposed to live on your catch!"

The storm was still holding its breath, and Tomaso went slowly over to his opponent, rocking his shoulders and rowing around in the air with his arms. He hissed at him:

"I won't even take in my mouth the name it's natural to call you, you plague-ridden rat, you insufferably stinking dog, you piece of carrion!"

"The town can never live from fishing!" replied the waiter. "You rotten toad, you dog turd! It's the cafes and the restaurants that we all live from. The tourists bring in the money!"

"You smell worse than a dead pig!" said Tomaso, holding his nose. Then he shouted at the top of his lungs: "Just notice how he stinks!"

Amid shouts of applause many of the fishermen held their noses as they loudly complained of the stink which emanated from their opponent.

"You're named Pasquale!" yelled Tomaso, intoxicated by his political success, "but you should really bear the name The Much-Stinking! Ha! I can't be bothered to do anything but laugh at you! You don't have the brains to carry a discussion forward to victory! And your smell is much too strong! It comes ahead of you and disproves your arguments."

The waiters looked chagrined at getting the worst of the exchange.

"We owe everything to the tourists," said Pasquale.

"I don't even want to sully my mouth by saying what I do on the tourists! Tomorrow we're building the harbor and doing our business on the tourists!"

Cheers. But the waiters now shouted very loudly, trying to be heard:

"The tourists bring money!"

"We shit on the tourists!"

"The tourists bring money!"

"Most highly honored waiters!" cried Tomaso ironically. "The tourists also bring much else! For example the unmentionable disease which Pasquale has caught from them!"

Wild hilarity, a sense of victory. Pasquale gulped:

"You do just fine with your own ugly and pernicious diseases, you dead pig!"

"Tomaso! Are we going to put up with him talking to us like that, just because we are poor fishermen?" said Timberio.

"No, no!" cried the fishermen.

"He is in truth an extremely low and vicious person!" shrieked Tomaso. "He wants to sell the town to the tourists!"

"Out with the tourists! Away with them! Away with them!"

"We want tourists! We want tourists!" yelled the waiters again, and there were more of them now.

"Before the tourists came, everyone was poor!" added Pasquale.

"Don't listen to that hard-hearted man!" replied Tomaso quick-wittedly. "He has even used his old sick dog to make spaghetti sauce for the tourists. I won't even take in my mouth the name of the vulgar, filthy sickness the dog died of!"

"Will you shut up?" yelled Pasquale in a fury. "It didn't have any such disease as you're thinking of! And besides it's not true, because it's a secret!"

"Oh, so you're lying, too!" rejoined Tomaso. "Your mother must have conceived you with the devil himself!"

"Fie on your disgusting mother!" roared Timberio.

"A monstrously loathsome and unhygienic mother!" crowed Tomaso.

"Ha!" yelled the attacked: "And I won't even name the name of your mother, Tomaso! Just so I won't humiliate you too much when people hear it! You would fall to the ground like a dead bird if I merely reminded you of your mother, it would bring such shame over you! When I think of your mother, I forget that you are my enemy, I feel as sorry for you as if you were another human being. Such a horrible wretch she was."

The waiters were shouting and dancing because suddenly their side was winning. "Hey, hey!" they shrieked.

"The cultural debate is in full swing," said Georg. We were all standing speechless, listening to the goings-on. Mario had long since left the bar, and was now standing on tiptoe, jumping with joy. He was on both sides at once, and clapped every time one of the debaters made a point.

For a moment Tomaso stood still under the attack. Then I saw that foam was collecting in the corners of his mouth. The rest happened so fast that it was over before anybody realized it, and no one saw the blow. But we heard it. A thud like the chop of an axe on Pasquale. A white flash in the air, a waiter's jacket flying. There he lay.

"Get the waiters!" boomed Timberio's voice. And for a few minutes the waiters were like white flakes of foam before the storm. Then they marshalled their forces, and Pasquale tried to get up. But

Timberio saw him and felled him with a formidable box on the ear. There he lay again, and someone upturned a table over him.

The waiters tried to form a front, but the fishermen drove them apart and vanquished them one by one.

"Hey, hey, hey!" yelled Mario: "Hit 'em! Hit 'em!"

One waiter brandished a fork and drove a fisherman to flight. "*Avanti*!" he shrieked. "Forward, hotel workers!" More followed his example and the fishermen retreated.

"They're not hitting each other for real!" shouted Mario:."Look! Look!"

Indeed the bloodshed did not measure up to the spectacle and the movement which was going on. We lamented the fact.

"Mario!" said Georg. "Do your duty and join in the fray!"

"Best of all *signori*, I am not of a combative nature."

The fight calmed down, but the lungs of the combatants got more air thereby, and the yells grew louder. Now and then a single oath detached itself from the mass and rose skyward like a flare.

"But you took part in the campaign in Greece?" said Georg.

"O Madonna, that was horrible! It's true that I was in the war over there."

"Is it also true that you carried a white flag on your belly under your uniform? To wave with?"

"Best of all *signori*," said Mario gravely, "I swear that it is true! The most intelligent of us had such flags concealed on our persons, and our mothers and sisters had made them with straps already sewn on, so that we could tie them to our gun barrels!"

"And armed with them you went forth into battle?"

"*Signore*, it was our firm intention to use the flags at the sight of the first Greeks."

"And it went well?"

"Yes, *signore*! The Greeks lay in wait for us, and they were most frightfully angry! Madonna, they were very, very angry!"

"It was a good thing that you had the flags, then?"

"*Signore*, it was extremely lucky that I had my flag, for I was the only one who had it handy. I had taken it out from around my waist ahead of time and was carrying it in my pocket. I raised it immediately, and we surrendered."

"The whole company?"

"All of us."

"So you were all saved?"

"Not one man was wounded, *signore!*"

"You should have got a medal!"

Mario looked down, grave and modest:

"That isn't the sort of thing you get decorated for in war, *signore!*"

Georg looked deadly serious, clutched his head and said:

"Lord, I wish I'd done the same!"

"You were wounded, *signore?*" said Mario sympathetically.

Everybody knows that Georg has shrapnel in his head and is disabled.

We were interrupted by a sudden hush falling over the piazza. After about a minute it was utterly still. The warring parties let go of each other, they stood side by side like brothers, they whispered cautiously among themselves, and they all stared in the same direction, up one of the narrow side streets which open into the Piazza del Sole.

As a faint, faint breeze steals through a wheat field, thus did a whisper go over the square: "O Madonna, *il professore!*" And: "Yes, it is him!" Or: "No, no, it's impossible!" But the buzzing mounted, apprehensive and skeptical: "*Il professore!* Yes, it is him!"

"What in the world is going on, Mario?" said Georg.

Mario had gone pale, and stole cautiously out onto the piazza so that he could see up along the street. We could follow the expression on his face through the whole gamut from disbelief to doubt to certainty, reverence and awe, up to plain terror.

"Yes," he whispered, "it is him! Madonna, it is him! *Il professore!*"

"Who is it, for heaven's sake?"

It did me good to look at Georg, who had kept his head. On the other hand Pamela failed utterly.

"Ugh, this is creepy!" she said and ran off.

Mario backed in our direction again, mumbling to himself.

"Well, tell us, man! Who is it?" I said.

"It is *il professore*, it is the *skald* Svensson! He's coming, O holy Mary, he's coming!"

"Who the hell is it?" said Georg. "Who *is* he?"

No reply from Mario. Silence on the square.

Awe and dread stood painted on every face, some of them furtively sneaked away, but most backed up against the walls so that a space opened in the center of the square. The odd audible sigh. A few hastily whispered words. They all showed the clearest signs of consternation.

"It is the poet Svensson," mumbled Mario and made a big sign of the cross over his chest. "He has lived here for more than twenty years."

"Impossible," said Georg. "I've never seen or heard of him."

"The poet Svensson hasn't been outdoors in sixteen years! O Madonna, he is a very great bard, a *grandissimo poeta* who hasn't been out in sixteen years!"

There was a rushing sound in the crowd, it gasped like water in a mighty torrent. The skald had drawn nearer.

"O ave Maria!" said Mario. "What can have happened?"

Now the people were shouting:

"Svensson! Svensson! *Il professore*! He's coming here! Oh, oh, he's coming! He's coming!"

It was getting on our nerves, and Georg shook Mario:

"But in God's name, man! What does he do if he doesn't go out?"

"Madonna, he writes poetry! And we bring him wine! That is our task."

"Why have I never seen him?"

"*Carissimo signore*, he never goes on the street. No foreigner has ever seen him. Eight years ago a commission came from his own fatherland to fetch him and take him home, but we didn't betray him. He is a very great poet, and we hid him so that they didn't find him. We will never betray him. Oh, a great poet! O Madonna, here he comes!"

Mario hid his face in his hands, and a storm rose up from the people. Many knelt.

An emaciated man, about six foot six, staggered onto the square. His beard and hair were thoroughly blond, and he walked with his eyes narrowed, squinting at the daylight. Two small boys with a wicker bottle and glasses followed, and a third went ahead and showed the poet the way. They walked as quietly and reverently as choirboys. Svensson's face was distorted with fury.

"Vere de hell iss my vine?" he shrieked. "Vy heff yew treeted me so nessty?"[1]*

Silence. Bowed heads.

"Vutt!" he went on. "Ken yew not enser? Vy heffn't yew brawt me my vine?"

He stared around and waved his arms. The sight of so many able-bodied men brought him to the edge:

"Yew picks! Go home! Go home! Pasqvale! Vere are yew?"

Pasquale was more or less on his feet again. "*Maestro*, here em I!"

"Vutt in hell iss going on? Vere are my fiftoon leeters?"

"At vunce! *Maestro, subito!*"

"Go avay! Effrybuddy go home!" He swept menacingly and fearsomely with his arms, and they understood him. They started sneaking around the corners of the houses and disappeared.

"All Satan's fishers to their deffilish boats! Paskvale, go home and fetch my curset vine!"

"Yess, at vunce, pest uff all brofessore!" He disappeared.

"Mario," I said, "How can Pasquale possibly understand Swedish?"

"Oh," he said, "*il professore* has forced several of us to learn a little Swedish, for he himself prefers to speak only the language of his own fatherland. I know a few words myself, for example: 'Town the hetch!' and, 'I heff no munny,' and, 'I kent bay,' and, 'Vere iss my vine?' And: 'Deffil take Mussolini!' And: 'Pring me fiftoon leeters!' And: 'Feend uff a mairchant Satan!'"

"Timperio! Go out and fish, yew deffil!"

Exit Timberio.

"Vutt the hell year iss it today?"

---

1. In the original Svensson speaks Swedish, which is intelligible to Norwegian readers.

"1958, pest of all brofessore!"

"The deffil, vutt a year!"

He had caught sight of us, and let his glance rest on Georg; there was recognition in his expression.

"Yew drunkert!" said the *skald* and pointed at him with his big, trembling hand.

Georg: "Yeah!"

The *skald* Svensson: "Brudder, gneiss brudder!"

It was friendship to the death at first glance. Georg got up, they fell toward each other, they tripped over themselves and spoke Swedish, German, and Latin:

"A sutherner from Skawnia, tralallala!" sang the bard.

> *"Freude, schöner Götterfunken,*
> *Töchter aus Elysium!"*

Rejoiced Georg:

> *"Wir betreten freudetrunken,*
> *Himmlische, dein Heiligtum...!"*

The three small boys stared at them with wide, pious eyes.

"Why is one of the boys carrying a kerosene lantern in his hand?" I said to Mario.

"It's a custom of *professore* Svensson since days of old," he replied. "Electricity and streetlights were first introduced in Bellapalma in 1942, and one must assume that the professor has so far not observed this step forward. In the old days it was difficult to venture out after dusk without a lantern."

While those two trod a measure on the boards Tomaso, without greeting me, came quietly over to the bar.

"Do you have them, *caro amico*?" he said to Mario.

"Yes, here they are!" Mario bent down and brought out a package wrapped in newspaper: "*Grandissimo pescatore*, you can count it yourself!"

"Thanks, I'll probably get in a new lot tonight. How many do you want, best friend of all?"

Mario considered.

"The tourists are coming soon," he said, "so I'll take all I can get."

"Twenty thousand?"

"As much as I can get, *grandissimo pescatore*!"

"*Buonissimo*, the problem is just to get them up here. But perhaps it'll work out this evening."

"I'll take everything I can get, *carissimo* Tomaso! Luckies and Camels and Chesterfields. I'd be glad for Pall Malls too."

"Fine."

"And then there was one more thing! Dear friend, I have a couple of messages for you, Tomaso. The two ladies...."

They put their heads together and whispered, and I rose discreetly and went up to the Hotel Paradise.

FOUR

Hotel Paradiso certainly deserves its name; nothing is spared to create a pleasant setting for guests wishing peaceful vacations in near-tropical surroundings. It is an Eden of orange trees, grapevines, peach trees, arcades, places to rest, ponds, tile floors and terraces. In the garden there is even a thriving banana palm in front of the prospect over the blue sea. Antique marble fragments, column stumps, sarcophagi and a couple of busts of Caesar also contribute to creating an atmosphere of soft, voluptuous idleness.

On the main terrace the table was set for all who were to take part in the meeting, and I was the last to arrive. After the almost oriental ceremonial courtesies we took our places. There were five of us—Police Chief Agnolino, Mayor Lambo, *Monsignor* Leone, tourist chief Strozzi, and me—aside from the host himself, the musical, good-natured, plumpish hotelkeeper Lippi. He remained standing at his place and took the floor:

"My very dearest sons of the town and highly excellent friends! Our small but very dear town's interests have made it necessary that we take steps to pacify the excited populace. As our ancestral town's most trusted and responsible men we are met together to seek counsel against the evil and monstrously asocial elements which now threaten to destroy the town's building of tourist lodgings, obstruct the hotel business, and thereby deprive the whole community of its economic foundation. In other words: *The fishermen must be stopped!*

"I won't waste many words explaining the insanity of the fishermen's plan to build a mole over the bay to create a harbor by the beach. No reasonable citizen will have difficulty seeing that this would mean Bellapalma's ruin; a harbor would completely destroy the beach for swimming, and it is precisely the beach which has now for many years been the source of the town's prosperity. The fishermen must be deflected from their monstrous project of the breakwater. The workers must again be put to their Christian, society-preserving work.

"We, gentlemen, are here to solve the problem. In short: Now good advice is at a premium!

"At the same time, *eccelentissimi signori*, there is no cogent reason to assume that we would master our task better if, during our ever-so-important meeting, we were to resort to fasting and abstinence from God's good gifts. I have planned for the body too to be considered during today's conference."

"Bravo!" rang out Father Leone's deep, resonant voice. I had been watching him during the hotelkeeper's introductory words, and had not succeeded in deciphering the expression on his face. Now I understood that it was hunger. Father Leone is an uncommonly good-sized man, well over six feet tall, and big-boned and muscular besides. His large, red face is imperturbable and dignified, but with flashes of kindness and sagacity. He is much beloved in the town, and no Bellapalman meets him on the street without kissing his hand with sincere devotion. His first word at our meeting, then, was "Bravo!"

Lippi went on:

"Dear friends, *reverendissimi signori*, first: mussel soup with Veronese white wine. After that a small, ever so small, but I believe I may venture to promise: *tasty* stew of langoustes, *scampi*, prawns, lobster. Again: white wine from Verona. Then a little filet mignon, this time with red wine, a good aged wine of my own from one of the best vintage years which it was given to my blessed father to live to see. Finally: a heady French wine with which the gentlemen will not be wholly unfamiliar, along with a bit of dessert consisting of candied fruits and divers cheeses, among them our local specialty of smoked sheep cheese from the mountains above Bellapalma.

"May the gentlemen enjoy the meal! Welcome to the table!"

Amid the general pleasure I heard Father Leone's carefree monk's laughter, which in its time had made him so popular at seminary. He joined Lippi's light voice in the old song:

> *Beve per nostri madre,*
> *beve per nostri padri!*
> *Che noi figli siamo,*
> *beviam*
> *beviam*
> *beviamo!*

We emptied our glasses, and gave the floor to Father Leone, as the most exalted person among the guests:

"This old drinking song witnesses to our forefathers' pious sense of the family as the sustaining force in society, along with the Church and its lowly servants. Let us salute our host for his celebrated cuisine!"

We emptied our glasses anew.

Lippi:

"And now will the speakers report in turn and present their wise and insightful proposals as to what in their opinion we must do next to save our little town from chaos and lawlessness and poverty."

Mayor Lambo was a very old man, but he insisted on giving his speech standing. It took him some time to get to his feet, and he upset his glass—which, luckily, was empty. Lambo first cleared his throat for a long time to make sure that he still had a voice, and then opened the discussion in a high, quavering old man's falsetto:

"Eh, eh! *Signori*! Hrm, hrm! Never before has there been in Bellapalma such unrest and unpleasantness as today. Brothers rise up against their fathers, brother against brother! Father against grandfather! The fishermen break with the natural order, hrm, hrm hrm!—and refuse to obey, yes refuse to obey! their, hrm hrm, divinely appointed authorities. Hrm. Mayor, priest and police chief are paralyzed in their duties. Hrm!! Disobedience and a rebellious spirit have broken out. The fishermen demand, O Madonna, *demand* that the resources of the town treasury be used to defray the expenses of the hrm, hrm, hrm! irksome construction of the ungodly breakwater which will ruin our little town. Hrm! The preliminary work on the godless breakwater is already begun, and when I tried to forbid them to go ahead half an hour ago, I hrm, hrm, hrm received the answer that I—"

He stopped quavering and made a few little squeaks in the air toward us. The police chief leaned toward him, and--also with a high, thin voice--quavered back:

"…that you…?"

"…that I could kiss…no, no! My honor forbids me to repeat it, but the esteemed gentlemen will understand *what* I was exhorted to, hrm, hrm, hrm! do."

He drew breath and his voice changed from falsetto to almost inaudible squeaks:

"I, I see in this rebellious spirit, this disobedience, this…this lawlessness…hrm, hrm, hrm! a sign that a new and godless time has made its entry into the old and pious town of Bellapalma. Insolence and self-will have invaded our little town."

He stopped and breathed again a few times, then raised his arms above his head and quavered with horrible force:

"It is *the times*, gentlemen, the *times*! Crime and rebellion have replaced the pious and upright life in Bellapalma. It's the *times*! The *Postwar era* stands before us and spits in our faces! Hrm, hrm, hrm! Religion and obedience have been trampled in the dust by the *times*! Hu, hu!

"What does your Reverence say to this, *Monsignor* Leone? Don't you agree with me, Leone?"

Father Leone had evidently been lost in his own thoughts, for he replied:

"By St. Luke, I certainly haven't tasted a mussel soup like this since I was a young curate in Bonassola! Oh, these little pearls of *frutti del mare*! These delicacies in their thin garlicky broth! And this wine, Lippi, oh, it's exceptional!"

He raised his glass.

"The *times*, reverend father," quavered Lambo, "the *times*!"

Leone didn't look at him, but followed the waiter with his eyes as he served the stew. They were two dark, shiny, benevolent eyes, and they were framed by big, black, arching eyebrows.

"We have plenty of time," he mumbled absently.

"Eh, heh!" squeaked Mayor Lambo, "the times are upon us! What shall we do, gentlemen, to drive out this new age which has forced its way into Bellapalma, with all its hrm, hrm, hrm! its boorishness and unrest to destroy the old harmony and set man up against God and the old values! Hrm, hrm, hrm! The old values!"

He waved around, gasped fretfully for air, and quavered:

"The old values! The old values! Hrm, hrm!"

He sank down, trembling and breathing heavily.

At the same instant Police Chief Agnolino rose—small and wind-dried, with running eyes; he was in full uniform, complete with saber, gold stripes and gold buttons. His wrinkled old face was browner than ever against his white moustache.

"Yes," he quavered, "the old values! I agree! We must keep to the old values!"

Agnolino's voice was even thinner and squeakier than the Mayor's had been. For that matter they resembled one another in many ways. He took a long, almost triumphant look around, then quavered his secret out into the world:

"Now, I think that it was terribly wrong of them to introduce this railway into Italy! I've been saying that forever! Way back in 1903—or was it 1902?—I said that this railway would never lead to anything good, but rather to crime and misery, and to—yes, yes, to the destruction of the old values."

His voice grew thinner and thinner as he squeaked:

"We should never have brought in the railway, Lambo! You're so completely right about that, *buonissimo* Lambo!"

"And then the telephone!" squeaked Lambo, "the telephone!"

"Terrible!" quavered Agnolino. "Just terrible! Not to mention the *long-distance telephone*!"

"Dreadful!" squeaked the other. "Oh, oh, just dreadful! And on top of that the *steamships*!"

"Yes, yes," continued Agnolino, "horrible, utterly wicked and horrible! But what I see as worst of all is the *airships*!"

"The balloons already showed that things were going to go wrong," cried Lambo. "The balloons already showed it!"

"Way back in '12, or was it in '13, or in '22, unless it was in '24, I said…yes, what was it I said…? I said that—yes, these airships, I said, they would destroy the old values!"

"The steamships!" creaked Lambo, "the cursed steamships!"

"Already when this, this Count Zeppelin fell down into the Rhine with his exasperating vessel, then I said it! That this wouldn't lead us forward! I'm not even sure that he's a real count, this Zeppelin, and they've been awfully quiet about him of late!"

Agnolino looked around triumphantly.

"Extremely quiet!" he concluded.

"The steamboats have been our misfortune," squeaked Lambo, "hrm, hrm!"

"And this Nobile, him I've never liked, gentlemen," quavered Agnolino. "I have always felt a strong aversion to him."

His old, sour-milk eyes rested disapprovingly on me.

"And this, this Roaldo Amundso, he is even a countryman of yours, *signore*!"

"Yes," I said, "and I've never been able to forgive him for the thing with the airships!"

Agnolino sank down into himself and collected his strength, then raised his head in a desperate effort. He drew himself up and whined:

"These damned airships! Stop the building of airships! I hate airships!"

"Don't shout so, best of all police chiefs," said Father Leone gently.

Mayor Lambo leaned forward toward the priest.

"Most reverend Father, doesn't Your Reverence agree that the steamboats are just as bad? What have they not meant, for example, for the steady expansion of immorality? Oh, St. Antonio, how I hate this immorality which is spreading among the young!"

Agnolino, that pious old man, admired for his manliness, looked malevolently at him.

"Airships!" he said.

"Hrm, hrm, hrm!! Steamboats!" harumphed Lambo.

Strozzi and Lippi now exchanged glances; both had made several attempts to get a word in, but had been hushed by the old men who, by dint of their grey hairs, were masters in the house. Father Leone was wholly unaffected, and ate and drank with a good appetite.

"They should never have brought in this, this railway!" said Agnolino. "I've always been against it."

Lambo said:

"*Signori*! Best of all friends! We have now hrm, hrm, hrm! worked our way forward to the center of what it's all about. And I must ask that one of the company, preferably Strozzi, now write down the separate points which are of the greatest significance!"

He raised the fingers on his left hand and tried to count on them, lifting them up toward the light to see them better.

"First there was: No. 1, the railway; then No. 2, the telephone; then No. 3..."

"The railway!" Agnolino chimed in. "Don't forget the railway!"

Lambo considered.

"Yes," he said, "I've included that. Now write, Strozzi! Write down the points!"

"Very best *signor* mayor..." Lippi tried to speak, but Lambo interrupted him:

"Then comes No. 3, the steamboats! Don't forget them! They are tremendously important, especially for Bellapalma, which lies by the sea! Do you have that, Strozzi, best of all tourist chiefs?"

"Yes," said Strozzi quietly.

"When do the airships come in?" squeaked Agnolino. "This Count Zeppelin! It's a shame!"

"Yes, yes, the airships!"

"I think we're on the wrong track," said Lippi heavily.

"We must put in the socialists!" cried Strozzi.

"Yes, yes," quavered Lambo, "and the communards! This Paris Commune has brought infinitely great misfortune with it!"

"Have you got the airships?" said Agnolino impatiently.

"Yes, and then evolution!" replied Lambo. "No. 4, the Communards. No. 5, evolution, No. 6 and No. 7…? We must have seven points if it's to make an impression."

"Write Darwin and materialism," said Father Leone.

"How infinitely glorious that we have monsignore with us! That may be the town's salvation, gentlemen!" cried Lambo. "It's most glorious that you are with us, Leone!"

Agnolino trembled and hiccupped with excitement:

"What is Darwin?" he whimpered.

Lambo looked at him and replied evasively:

"A very bad Darwinist!"

"Did he have anything to do with the airships?" persisted Agnolino.

"Hrm," replied Lambo, "one can safely say that…that…without Darwin practically nothing would have come of the airships."

"Then I'm against him!" squeaked the police chief. "Write him down!"

And Darwin was written down.

"This isn't getting us anywhere," said Lippi. "I'm afraid that…."

He was interrupted by Lambo:

"And this monstrously naughty materialism, Strozzi, write it down!"

Strozzi wrote, cultured and well brought up, but without enthusiasm in his eyes.

"That'll impress the fishermen!" crowed Lambo.

But Agnolino wanted to say something, and we waited until he had drawn breath. He surprised us.

"No," he quavered, "it's too long a list, it has so many words that I'm afraid it will go over the fishermen's and the workmen's heads."

I looked admiringly at Father Leone, who was eating with unbroken appetite while he emptied glass after glass. He seemed wholly indifferent to what was happening around him.

I too ate well.

Strozzi looked up from the paper with his big shiny squirrel's eyes. He blinked a couple of times, carefully stroked his little black moustache, and said cautiously:

"Most honored gentlemen, I fear that we may possibly be on the wrong track."

"Now let me read our seven points," said Agnolino without regarding him. Instead the old man stood up and supported himself against the table with one hand while he held the paper in the other. We were now at the filet and the red wine. We clearly heard Father Leone grumble:

"These motorboats are a curse, nowadays you never get fresh fish anymore. In the old days, by St. James the Elder! there was so much fresh fish that you could reconcile yourself to a Christian lifestyle. Oh, the most delicious things you could imagine! The wine was better, too. Aye, aye, it was first-class in those days! Nothing is what it used to be. I won't even mention the decline of theology."

Agnolino's shaking hand rustled the paper, then his thin childlike voice began the reading:

"*Reverendissimi signori*! I read: 1) the Railway, 2) the Telephone, 3) Steamboats, 4) Airships—yes, airships, yes!—5) the Communards, 6) Darwin, this Darwin, yes—and finally 7) materialism."

"Bravo! Bravo!" squeaked Lambo.

Agnolino gripped the tablecloth tightly to keep himself upright. He continued:

"Best of all gentlemen! Now that all have had their say, I shall present my further proposal.

"If those present think that the list won't be too, too extensive for the fishermen's capacity for abstraction, then we can keep the seven points despite everything—inasmuch as we are therein sticking to the root of evil—and undertake a public reading of these same points on the piazza in front of Alexi's trattoria, where the rebellious elements will have gathered. We have now discerned the reasons, of which I myself especially wish to emphasize this, this railway, along with the airships and mat—well, the gentlemen know what I'm thinking of,—and we have now the full right to repel force with force. We know what must be driven out of our beloved little town, and I will meet with the entire mobile police force, armed, at Alexi's trattoria, and under the protection of these easily maneuverable police I will read our seven points to the fishermen. I presume that this must bring them to reflection and reason.

"If, however, it does not bear the desired fruits, I will unhesitatingly take the next step, namely the reading of the riot act, and will have the restless elements arrested!"

"Bravo! Bravo!" quavered Lambo.

"With that, gentlemen," said Agnolino, "the matter should be settled, and so we will accept my proposal, since there were no other suggestions. So first I myself will undertake a refutation of this Darwin out on the piazza, and after that mat…mat… materialism in general, and if the people still haven't seen the error of their ways, they shall taste the strong arm of the law!"

He looked down at his saber to be sure he had it with him.

"My motion is then carried."

To my astonishment he now turned to me.

"Most eminent, most highly esteemed *professore!* What is your opinion?"

"*Carissimo, eccelentissimo* police chief, I am wholly on your side in this matter. I have great faith in the effect your words will have on the rebels."

Father Leone raised his big red face and sent me a cold and wide-awake look. He said nothing, but it was unpleasant. Now Strozzi arose with desperate resolution in his friendly brown eyes.

"*Signori,*" he said, "I too have a proposal to make."

Lambo and Agnolino looked commiseratingly at each other and groaned.

"Yes, yes," creaked Lambo, "We could hardly expect anything else!"

"As Chief of the Tourist Bureau in Bellapalma this matter weighs very heavily on my heart...."

Agnolino now whispered loudly to Lambo:

"I, I think that my proposal is much better. Just listen to how badly he expresses himself."

"The tourist season is upon us, everything must be ready to receive the unsuspecting flood of tourists when it arrives in earnest. A revolution *must* be averted. The houses must be ready, the beach must be clear, everything must be in order, and above all: *the atmosphere must be good*! The waiters and the fishermen and the workmen must all be happy and satisfied, all must be peace, harmony, lightheartedness and joy, just as the tourists expect of Bellapalma. After all, we know that the town's carefree life, the natives' good-natured innocence, their smiles and friendliness are priceless treasures in the service of the tourist trade. We must see to it that some of the bearers receive timely payments from us to surprise the tourists by declining to be paid for some helping hand, we must organize the everyday life from the ground up so that this year too it goes straight to the foreigners' hearts. Everything must be prepared, the folk songs must be rehearsed anew, the fishing boats must be freshly painted, the children must be drilled in giving old ladies flowers without accepting money for them. In short: The morale must be of the highest. This year as always!"

"Yes, said Leone, "the morale, then! So sing a little, Lippi!"

"Another time, *Monsignore*. Not now!"

But Father Leone persisted, with the authority which both his office and his deep, lovely voice gave him:

"Yes, sing, Lippi! Sing one of the folk songs you learned at hotel management school! The one about your being without mother and father, that's such a lovely song! What have we got back for sending you to hotel management school when you were only a snot-nosed little waiter's apprentice, if you can't even sing one of the songs for us?"

"Best, *reverendissimo* Father! Another time!" said Lippi pleadingly.

But the prelate persisted regardless, his eyes sparkling, his face growing redder. He was almost like a man who had been drinking wine.

"So sing a more jolly one, then! *Per esempio* this one: 'Jambi, jambi! O la la la la! Jambi, jambi! O la la la la! Funiculi, funicula, funiculi, funicula!' And you don't have your tambourine with you, either!"

"Most outstanding and excellent Father, let me off just for now! Time is short, *Monsignore*!" Lippi implored him. From outside we could now hear noise and yells, as if from an agitated crowd. Strozzi went on with his speech:

"Your pardon, most highly esteemed *signori*! But I have not yet come to my proposal."

"Let's hear!" said Lippi.

"If we absolutely must," quavered Agnolino, turning to Lambo to groan over the tourist chief.

"Hm, yes, what I wanted to say was…" said Strozzi, "that hm, my idea is perhaps a bit daring.…"

"So speak up, then, man!" Lambo squeaked sternly.

"Well, I want to propose that…hm, it's difficult to find the right words for it.…"

The noise from the street was now amounting to a disturbance.

"Even if your idea isn't as good as mine, we'll still be glad to listen to it," said Agnolino. "Just speak up, my young friend!"

"Well, I wanted to propose…excuse me, but this may sound a bit malapropos, gentlemen, I propose that.…"

I looked at the tourist chief and hardly recognized him. Was this the always confident, always smiling Strozzi? Should he be standing here groping for words? Was it really possible that the authority which emanated from the elders and the priest could paralyze him so completely?

"I can't say it, gentlemen," concluded Strozzi, blushing.

"My young friend, I can well imagine that your proposal lies on another plane, so to speak, than mine!" squeaked Agnolino indulgently.

"If you can't speak, then sing!" said Father Leone.

"May I whisper it?" asked Strozzi.

"Yes, said Agnolino, "do that. That may be the best!"

"In *signore* Lippi's ear?"

"Very well."

He went over to the hotelkeeper and whispered in his ear for a long time, while Lippi listened with mounting interest.

"Hell and damnation!" he said. "*Fifty* of them?"

"Yes," said the tourist chief.

"This is quite certain?"

"Yes, extremely certain and sure."

"This afternoon?"

"Yes."

"Then we're saved!" exalted Lippi. "This is marvelous! Yes, by St. Anthony, this is utterly glorious! Now the drinks are on me! Wine all around!"

More commotion, more yelling and screeching from outside.

"What kind of a most ungodly racket is this in the middle of the day?" whined Agnolino furiously. "I must investigate."

"Wait a little, *signori*!" cried Lippi. "You have to hear this! But it must be kept utterly secret. For it should come as a surprise, eh, Strozzi?"

"Yes, absolutely!"

Strozzi and Lippi bent down over each his old man's hairy ear and whispered for a long time. Leone went on eating cheese, enjoying the wine.

"That was indeed a strange proposal!" said Lambo. "It must truly be called hrm, hrm, hrm, strange."

Agnolino: "Most remarkable. One of the most remarkable I've heard. It was certainly better than I had expected of you, excellent tourist chief."

Lambo: "But tell me, doesn't this mean promoting immorality?"

Agnolino: "Of course it does! There's no possible doubt of that. And today we have resolved to combat materialism and immorality among the fishermen!"

"Fifty!" squeaked Lambo. "That's quite a few!"

"It ought to be enough," said Lippi thoughtfully.

Agnolino quavering, but satisfied: "Fifty will do very well."

"I'm worried about what *Monsignore* will say to this," squeaked Lambo. "I'm not sure that he will find it altogether moral to advance such a proposal."

Lambo bent down and sprayed gravy in Father Leone's large ear. The man of God listened attentively, with one eye closed, the other halfway open.

"Ai, ai," said he. "Fifty of them!"

Lambo whispered some more, and the priest considered.

"Yes," said he, "*dreadfully* immoral!"

Silence on the terrace. Everyone looked disappointed.

"But it's a brilliant idea!" continued Father Leone. "An utterly splendid idea which absolutely must be carried out."

They had all forgotten me, and just then a veritable storm broke loose outside. The crowd was in an uproar.

On the terrace too this pervasive unrest broke out. Everyone got up, even Leone finished his meal and wiped his mouth thoroughly with his napkin.

"If only they come soon!" yelled Lippi.

"You have to reckon with delays," shouted Strozzi. "Anything can happen. These days."

Agnolino stood up and shrieked:

"Pietro! Paolo! Come here! Come here! Pietro! Paolo! Idiots! Cretins! Miserable wineskins! Where are you?!"

The *carabinieri* must have been standing inside the door to the terrace, for now they were suddenly present, both of them heavily armed and with rifles over their shoulders.

"Get going!" squeaked Lambo. "The town must be saved! Get going!"

They were all at the door. The next minute I was alone on the terrace. No one had bothered to answer my question, fifty of what. I was completely forgotten.

It was late in the afternoon, and soon the first signs of dusk would appear. I left the hotel and walked rapidly down to the beach, through the swarming, agitated town.

FIVE

The wind was still faint, but southerly—and so warm that it brushed like a breath around my face and hands. Down on the beach I saw nobody, and went over to Giuseppe's boat where it lay drawn up beside all the blue and yellow and red fishing boats. I looked around once more, then hurriedly clambered up into the boat, lay down on the floorboards, and kicked off my shoes.

It was good to lie thus and look up at the sky, which was beginning to acquire a deeper shade of blue, and where the very first stars would become visible in a few minutes. I lay for a while in thought, and I recalled a conversation I had had with Georg when he was sober a few days back. I had been complaining to him, and had quoted a Norwegian poet:

"Every glad hour you have on earth shall be paid for with sorrow," I had said to him, and Georg replied:

"That's only half the truth, Anso!"

I: "And the other half?"

"Every painful hour you have on earth shall be paid for with sorrow," said Georg plaintively.

"What?" I said, thinking that I had heard wrong.

"Anso!" said Georg, "both joy and pain shall be paid for with sorrow. Learn that! It might be good for you to know."

"That's a hell of a view of life!" I said.

Georg looked at me before he replied:

"You are *troppo bambino*, Hans. You're just a little child."

"What in the world does it mean, then?" I mumbled.

"Do you know why we get along so well down here on the southern tip of the European continent?"

"No—?"

"It's because the population is so melancholy. An unbroken sadness lies over all this ancient landscape. In three thousand years these people have learned what life is like, and they've come to understand it . The sadness already begins in France, and the further south you come, the more mournful people get. Only east of the Rhine and on the wrong side of the Alps are people happy, and that's because it takes a couple thousand years to learn this wisdom. All the Latin peoples are melancholy, only the barbarians are happy. Look at a South Italian or even a Frenchman when he's standing alone in the evening and staring in front of him with a cigarette in the corner of his mouth, and notice the sorrow in the whole way he stands and in his whole expression!

"You may object that folk in the south are known precisely for their carefreeness and their constant guitar playing, their laughter, and their smiles?

"But that's tourist wisdom, Anso! It's a travel poster! They live on it! It's partly like that, but there's something else too. It's true that they jabber and shout and laugh and sing when they're together, but look at them when they're alone! Look at them in the evening!

"It's precisely because of their bottomless melancholy that they're so glad for a chance to laugh. That's why they're so fond of greeting each other in three hundred different ways, that's why they're so fond of a cheery answer. It's the only thing that makes their sorrow easier to bear. They've had all the blessings of civilization here for three and a half thousand years, and they've learned their lesson, and know that there's only one thing you can do with life to improve it. Learn that, Anso: All cultured folk are sad, only barbarians are happy.

"The sole thing you can do with your sorrow and with life's general incurability is to concentrate on the eternal joys: on wine, food, lovely weather, on the cool of the evening, on a folk song from the mountains, on greeting people cheerfully. The loveliest of all Italian greetings is one you may not even know, and it's only used when one passes someone sitting on the steps or the sidewalk to enjoy the cool of the evening. It goes: *"Buon fresco!"*—that is, "Good cooling!" and you might say it's the sum of all wisdom about what good you can wish a fellow human being on earth. You shouldn't demand too much, Anso!

"An intelligent people can learn a lot in three thousand years.

"That's why we get along so well down here. People spend their lives greeting each other. We feel more at home when we can sit quietly on the stump of a column from the earliest Greek colonization than when we visit our own countries up north. Our physical ancestry is not the same as our spiritual ancestry. After all, this whole south Italian region is actually Greater Greece, and we're born with all that mournful wisdom about life: that as a whole it can't be mended, all we can do is be content with putting Band-Aids on it."

"And then?" I said.

"We can keep our heads clear," he said.

"Why on earth do we need clear heads?" I said.

"To keep our cheerfulness."

"And then?"

"There isn't any more."

I lay on my back in the boat and thought about Georg's wisdom. The sky up there was on its way to becoming dark blue, but the warmth in the air was the same. Two small stars were visible, and beside me lay a wine bottle from Giuseppe's last fishing trip. I picked it up and sniffed it to make sure that it didn't contain water. Then I took a long swig from it and put it down again. Georg is no Faust, I said to myself. Then I heard someone rustling between the boats, and raised myself on my elbow, figuring the wait was over. But I was wrong; judging from the sounds there must be two people sneaking about. Then I heard Tomaso's voice:

"O Madonna! You are an extremely beautiful woman!"

To this Marie replied, with her lovely English *r*'s and diphthongs: "Oh, Thomaso!"[2]

Tomaso: "You are so frightfully pretty! And I have burned with an extremely painful love for you ever since you came here! Maria, I've lived a very terror-filled life, worse than in Purgatory, of sheer burning love! You are just like the vast shining sun itself, and other women are not even like the exceedingly wretched electric bulbs in comparison with you! O Madonna, how I despise those other, altogether paltry women! Ha, I wouldn't even look at them if they all came here and went down on their knees at once! To me they're like terrible stinging nettles, but you are an extremely beautiful girl! You smell like many flowers and like delicious food! O Marie!"

"Oh, Thomaso, why do you have so little time?" whispered Marie.

"Madonna! My time is not my own today, for I must lead the fight to get the breakwater built. I must stand up to the evil and cold people who hate the honest fishermen. Afterwards I'll have lots and lots of time, most beautiful Marie, and we shall be together always!"

Now they took a flaming leave of each other, and Tomaso said:

"Most beautiful of women, you must do me a service! Will you in your colossally great goodness take a suitcase for me up to the Sunshine Bar? There are only a few clothes in it, but you must give it to Mario! My palm, my rose, best of all my friends, will you do this for a little worm of a fisherman?"

Marie moaned with bliss:

"Let me heft it, Thomaso."

"Here, fairest of girls!"

"It's not the least bit heavy!"

"O Madonna! Now I must be parted from you! My heart does not want to, but my head says that I must! Oh, oh! I'm like to die!"

"Oh, Thomaso! Oh!"

I heard by her footsteps that she was leaving, but I lay still and waited. In a few minutes there was a whistled signal, but not the right one. Some almost inaudible steps, and then Tomaso:

2. The variant spelling is meant to indicate the aspirated t of English as opposed to the unaspirated t of Italian. —Tr.

"O Madonna! Oh, you extremely lovely, you most glorious woman! Oh, I have waited for you, and as I waited I was in a hell of longing! Oh, in truth a terrible burning, flaming hell!"

And now Pamela's voice, also with Anglo-Saxon *r*'s and diphthongs, but with the broader, at once nasal and gurgling pronunciation which for so long has hampered relations between the US and Great Britain:

"Oh, Thomaso, darling!"

"My dove, my rose, my flaming, O extremely flaming love! O you who are vastly much more marvelous than other women!"

"Oh, Thomaso! Oh, you're lovely. . . ."

On principle I have nothing against a little eavesdropping now and then, but this was too much, and I'd lain there long enough now. I held my hands over my ears to avoid hearing more, as I watched the sky darken above me. More and more stars appeared.

For a while I lay thus with my hands over my ears and was at peace, and the sight of Venus put me in a quiet and pensive mood. I had to lie utterly still so as not to be heard, and though I longed to empty the bottle beside me, I had to let it be. And since I was forced to keep my body completely quiet, I fell into temptation and began to think. I brooded for a while over why life was as it was, and not more enjoyable, and why I was always writing and writing and plaguing myself morning, noon and night— as if the sun couldn't rise without my help! It would be much more pleasant to write some nonsense or other for the newspapers, something so foolish that everybody agreed with it, and would willingly pay good money to read their own opinion in print. Something about progress and underdeveloped countries and down with illiteracy and God knows what. Then I would only need to write for three or four days a month and could drink red wine and lie in the sun and read books the rest of the time. But I couldn't do that. The unrest was upon me, I wrote and wrote.

This made me sad, and I thought of my friends far away. I thought of Barbarossa, the great painter who laughed at himself and set his own life at naught and bummed around Europe in an old wreck of a car, now in Flanders, now in the Pyrenees, now in the mountains of Calabria, always on the road to nowhere. Why wasn't he here now? I felt bitter toward him. I missed him. Why wasn't he here, laughing his great lion's laughter, cheering me up, emptying wine bottles and telling his awful lying tales? Hell, what were friends good for if they were never around? And The Girl? Was she gone too? What would those two say to each other if they met? It would doubtless be uproar and carousing and guitar playing and yarning and absurdity at first sight!

But now Tomaso must be finished with Pamela. I unstopped my ears and listened.

"…O Madonna! I'll have lots of time once we're finished with our terrible fight for the breakwater. Pamela, you are infinitely more beautiful than that cold and extremely stuck-up English lady! Only one little finger of yours is like an immensely heavenly flower. I won't even bother to compare you with some of those other women, they're like dead beasts next to you!"

"Oh, Thomaso! Darling, you're so lo-o-ovely!"

He was all fire and flame.

"The stars in that wretched little sack of a heaven over us are merely as small, immensely filthy lice compared with you! Oh, Pamela, you most lovely of all women, I must ask you for a favor already this evening! I despise myself, I'm a rotten dog of a Neapolitan, because I have to ask you for something!"

"What is it, Thomaso?"

"I have a suitcase which is supposed to go up to Mario in the Sunshine Bar, but I can't take it up myself because I must go to a secret meeting. Can you, *O bellissima amica mia*, carry the suitcase up for me?"

Pamela was strong, and splendidly fitted for carrying suitcases. My respect for Tomaso rose steadily.

"Here, O beautiful friend! Is it heavy?"

"No, nothing!"

Pause and breathing. Pamela:

"Adieu, Thomaso - o - o! Oh! Until tomorrow!"

"Fairest of all the women who have set foot in this wretched land! The suitcase contains clothes, and must be delivered to Mario himself, to no one else!"

Leave-taking, silence, the end. Dark starry night, stillness.

I lay and waited, then it came. Tomaso, whispering:

"*Professore*, best of all professors! Are you there?"

"Tomaso! You best of all fishermen, exceeding great fisherman, *buonissimo* and *carissimo pescatore*! Here I am!"

He came over to the boat and stuck his head over the rail.

"*Grandissimo* cousin *professore!* How do you think it's going?"

"*Buonissimo* cousin Tomaso, *eccelentissmo!* It exceeds my wildest expectations! I admire you for your *intelligentissimo* solution to the transport problem!"

"*Carissimo professore!* By God, these two women are very bad and evil people, but still they both agreed to carry suitcases. And how did the fight in the square look today? Do you think it was satisfactory?"

"Cousin Tomaso, *reverendissimo amico*! The fight was splendid! No one could have done it better!"

Tomaso's face was black as night, but his teeth gleamed in the moonlight. He picked up a package wrapped in newspaper.

"Best of all cousin professors, here they are! You yourself shall have sixty percent of them, and I forty. On top of that you shall get back the money which you invested in buying the goods!" He opened the package and took out a fat bundle of notes. "Look here, cousin professor!"

"*Carissimo* Tomaso!" I said, "I'd sooner die than accept sixty percent. Don't enrage me, Tomaso! I'll take forty, and you, best of all cousin fishermen, shall have sixty for yourself!"

"*Buonissimo professore*, now listen to reason and don't be a *bambino*. Take the sixty percent! What, best of all cousins, would I, a louse of a fisherman, do with so much money?"

"Tomaso," I said, "my *carissimo* cousin and first-class fisherman! You're a dirty Roman, a civil servant and a landlubber, if you try to force sixty on me. I won't respect you for that! And I utterly refuse to take more than forty!"

"*Grandissimo professore*, I'll throw the money in the water if you don't want it. I think you should have sixty percent and your investment back! Otherwise I won't take anything!"

"Cousin Tomaso! I refuse, and you're making me sick and mad with rage! Not a lire more than forty percent!"

"I don't want more than that either, *professore*! Then what shall we do with the remaining twenty? *O caro professore*, now don't be a *bambino*! To write your works you need the material independence which the money can give you! Here, take it!"

"Tomaso, you talk like a dog and a heathen, like a wretched Sicilian. I don't want more than my share! If need be I can extend myself to take half, on condition that you yourself keep the other half! Now really, you've annoyed me long enough, and kept me with your chatter for much too long!"

He sent me a friendly look and said:

"*Carissimo professore*! I note that you are an educated man, and I yield. We'll split the bundle!"

"*Bravissimo* cousin, you're just magnificent!"

He picked up the bundle of notes and divided them by eye, weighed both piles in his hands and gave me one. I was satisfied, and stuck the bundle in my back pocket, which it padded out blessedly well. I lay back down on it and said:

"O exceedingly splendid *pescatore*, my favorite cousin, such a mass of bills is a great delight and a joy to lie on!"

He offered me a cigarette and lit them for us both.

"*Professore*," he said, "you are a good person and I respect you more than the whole town of Bellapalma! Can't you please tell me a little from your country?"

"About what, *buonissimo pescatore*?"

"About the fishermen, *car'amico*, about how they set out from land and mock the storm and laugh at the elements' most terrible fury. I like so uncommonly much to hear you tell about them, and about how many fish they catch, and how much money they get when they sell them at a price they've fixed themselves. Please, *professore*, tell me a little!"

"Dearest Tomaso, I think you've gone completely out of your mind. At an hour like this, when the fishermen are gathered at Alexi's and are just waiting for you before they begin in earnest! I'm shocked at you, Tomaso!"

The glow at the corner of his mouth intensified, and the gleam of the cigarette was mirrored in his shiny teeth.

"*Carissimo professore*, only a little bit! About how it is when the storm howls and the water freezes to ice in your hair and beard!"

"Tomaso, you are stark raving *lunatico*! I've never in my confused and idiotic life heard the like of such frivolous talk! Will you let them sit up there waiting for you?"

"Well, they can't start without me, *professore*! I'm the only one who can stir them up and make them discontented in the right fashion. Without Tomaso *niente revoluzione*! That's how it is, cousin *professore*. Just a little snatch of a story?"

I drew myself up to a sitting position, I was so mad at him.

"Tomaso," I said, gnashing my teeth, "you are the most immoral cretin I've ever seen! How would the world be if people were like you? If Lenin and Hitler and Musse and Stalin had been such vastly bad and evil people as you, what would have happened to the revolutions in the world? *Malissimo*! Tomorrow I'll tell you about all my Norwegian countrymen's colossally brave struggle on the ocean until you shit your pants with terror! But now I'm going up to the piazza!"

I stood all the way up, stuck my feet in my cloth-top shoes and jumped down onto the sand beside him in the dark. I took him by the hand.

"*Bravissimo pescatore*, now the fun begins! Good luck!"

"*Professore*, best of all professors, one question, just a small question?"

"Yes, very dearest Tomaso!"

"*Professore*, this other gentleman, *signore* Arnold. . . you know. . . do I have to hit him any more today?"

"*Buon pescatore*," said I, "there's 'have to' and 'have to'. It's not easy to say for certain. But I think we can leave it to chance a little, so that you only hit him if it works out that way, if it looks natural, that is. So that it seems to happen of itself. That will look best."

He wanted to come with me up to the town, but I stopped him.

"*Buonissimo* Tomaso, you must wait here at least five minutes! No one must see us together tonight."

He nodded with comprehension and smiled as he leaned his broad shoulder against the boat. He was standing like that when I left.

On the way I felt in my back pocket and let my fingers slip around and between the soft, lovely banknotes. For me they meant peace and quiet and independence with my next book—a tranquil life of study and hard work. As I climbed the stairs in the best possible humor, I made up a poem:

> Mild are the children of men in the south,
> Where they grow such excellent wine
> That you drink yourself daily to wisdom and truth,
> And become like the sun in your mind!

SIX

The piazza outside Alexi's was well lit by the big electric lamps and by the light from a couple of the bars there. Because of the heat all the doors and windows were open, and people sat in their shirtsleeves at the tables on the square. An unusually large crowd had assembled, particularly fishermen and laborers, but also all kinds of citizens of the town, a few waiters, some artisans, and nearly all the vagrants, idlers, and beggars which Bellapalma had. There were many children, a few women, a couple of transient tourists, but almost none of the town's resident foreigners. Over the door of the trattoria you could clearly read *Zi' Alexi*, "Uncle" Alexi, and inside his place the fishermen were gathered; only now and then did someone go out or in through the door. There was an atmosphere on the piazza which you could have cut into with a knife, and everyone felt that it was loaded to the breaking point. Something *would* happen in the course of the evening. People were speaking more softly than usual. No shouts, no laughter, just mumbling, soft words and fast, whispered messages.

At one of the tables Arnold sat alone, conversing quietly with a waiter who stood beside him. I went over and sat down at his table. Arnold looked bad, his eye was swollen, but he wasn't wearing dark glasses. Pamela must have forgotten to buy them, and now here he sat, keeping abreast of events. There is something brave, something indomitable about Arnold. He was pale.

"Well," I said, "how are the domestic politics coming along?"

"A madhouse," he replied bitterly, "an utter madhouse!"

"Can you tell me," I said, "why Bellapalma in particular should *not* be a madhouse?"

"Imagine," he said, "the whole business is being led by this illiterate Tomaso! It's actually an *illiterate* who has organized the whole thing!"

"Arnold," I said, "all deeper interest in politics presupposes a touch of illiteracy. To adopt a real political party line you must be capable of greatly simplifying all questions; you must teach yourself to believe that all misery is due either to the communists, or the fascists, or parliamentarism, or the Jews, or the bankers or the vegetarians or whatever. If you can't oversimplify you have no political clout. Every educated person knows that you politicians are brothers in sin and misery whether you are fascists or communists, or pinkos, or...."

"Shut up, Anso! You're a political incompetent, and you have no idea how serious these things are."

"Yes, I do," I said. "I know very well how serious they are, but the reason they've *gotten* so serious is because you politicos are the way you are. You have to learn, Arnold! Just learn!"

A loud, forceful voice rang over the piazza. It was the big red-haired fisherman Timberio, standing in Alexi's doorway shouting:

"Hallo! Now we're all here! We can start the meeting! Come on, we're going in!"

"Tomaso's not here!" called a fisherman. "No one has seen him!"

"Then we'll begin without him!" roared Timberio.

"Can't we wait a few minutes and see if he comes?"

But then Tomaso's own voice sounded through the crowd, and everyone turned toward the street which leads down to the beach. There he came, with swaying shoulders and a cigarette in the corner of his mouth. He waved soothingly with a brown hand.

"Here I am. Now we'll start!"

Tomaso pushed forward to the door and waved again.

"Come on!" he cried, "We have a lot to accomplish, *signori* fishermen!"

Those who were still outside now began to push past him through the door into the trattoria. Arnold stared at him, pale and furious, and for the first time I saw with my own eyes what is so often described in novels: his nostrils quivered. Arnold looked like a French general at the moment he decides to throw his army into a new defeat.

"He must be stopped!" he hissed, and took a breath.

"Arnold!" I said earnestly, laying a hand on his arm, "I must absolutely advise you against doing anything. He doesn't like you! In his eyes you are an evil and cold person who hates the honest fishermen."

"Disgusting fascist!" said Arnold indignantly.

"Only fishermen are allowed!" a furious voice rang across the square. It was one of the fishermen, who had caught a waiter in the act of sneaking into Alexi's. Timberio took the culprit and threw him out again with a roar.

"Away with you, Giuglio! We don't want spies in here!"

Timberio looked imposingly around the square, as if he were watching out for more interlopers.

"Have all the fishermen come in? *Signori pescatori*, are you all inside? Are there more? No more *pescatori*!"

He turned and went in, closing the door carefully after him. It was quiet again on the piazza.

Deathly quiet.

"Arnold," I said pleadingly, "there are two ways of writing indecently in our time. One way is to write about politics, the other is to write about sex. The first is vulgar, and the second is outmoded. You've fallen for both, and neither is your sphere. If you stop writing about these two things you'll have a chance to get rid of all your public and most of your readers, and you can start writing about serious subjects, about what really concerns you, Arnold!"

For a moment he looked at me with something like uncertainty in his eyes, but then his face resumed the barricade-expression.

"It's a duty," he said. "In today's world both political and sexual relations are atrocious, and it is my duty to work for a better future."

But that little glimpse had given me hope for him; I knew now that the prospect of being rid of his readers had moved him.

"Arnold, listen! You write about politics instead of people, and about sex instead of love. If you were to stop this, then you could get down to business and maybe write something sensible in the course of time."

"Nonsense!" he said.

"Arnold! Can't you at least refrain from getting mixed up in what's happening in Bellapalma, then? You could get into real trouble, and you only make matters worse by joining in."

"I follow my conscience!"

"All right," I said, "if you must save the republic, then in God's name you'll just have to do it! If you won't listen, then I daresay you'll feel it instead."

"What the hell do you mean by that?"

"Well, now, you've already tangled with Tomaso earlier today, and I think that in the name of decency you ought to show a grain of natural cowardice."

"There's no use trying to scare me, Anso."

Now a foaming sound spread over the piazza; Police Chief Agnolino was arriving under the escort of Pietro and Paolo. The *carabinieri* had their guns in their hands, and we all held our breath. It looked repulsive and fascist.

"There are your allies," I said.

"Shut up!"

The police chief and the *carabinieri* were followed by Lippi and Strozzi. Agnolino screeched in loud falsetto:

"Where are they? Where are the fishermen?"

He looked toward the trattoria and the locked door.

"Ha, here they are, and they've locked themselves in! Police forward!"

He sent Pietro and Paolo before him: "Open the door!"

No answer. The two of them stopped a ways from the door and looked around as if desire was lacking.

"Forward march!" squeaked Agnolino. "Knock! Knock! I say. Will you knock!"

He dragged himself after them. "Knock on the door, for the devil's sake! Oh, by St. Antonio, what scaredy-cats!"

Pietro carefully approached the door, raised his hand with a fierce expression on his face, but let it fall again and turned to Paolo.

"Can't you knock?"

"Knock yourself!" said Paolo.

"Why does it always have to be me?"

"You're standing closest, stupid!"

Agnolino now rolled his eyes wildly and waved his arms at the sky.

"O Madonna! Knock! Will you knock!" he snarled.

Again Pietro raised a hand, but sank into thought and stood motionless with his hand in the air.

"Yes," he said, turning his head, "but they might open."

Agnolino clenched his small brown fists threateningly.

"Will you knock, you coward? Knock! Knock!"

Now Pietro turned his back to the door and let his hand fall.

"Very dearest, *reverendissimo* police chief! Can't you knock yourself?"

Muted merriment on the piazza. Agnolino furious:

"You're fired as of tomorrow, you loathsome bastard, if you don't knock at once!"

Pietro turned resignedly, bowed his head and rapped faintly on the door. There was no answer.

"They're talking so loud in there," he explained.

"Knock harder, you Sicilian!"

Now Pietro knocked loudly on the door and took three rapid steps backward. He waited. We all waited. No sound came from inside that could be construed as a reply. Agnolino shrieked:

"Knock properly! Can't you just knock, you greatest of all idiots?!"

But Pietro turned to face him, and now he was angry and his teeth and eyes glittered.

"Now surely Paolo can knock for a bit!"

The people on the piazza nodded and mumbled that they were on Pietro's side in this question.

"Paolo!" quavered Agnolino. "Forward and knock! But hard."

Cringing, Paolo stepped forward and beat hard on the door. Pause.

"Knock even harder! Like that, yes, finally! That's good!"

The piazza resounded with the blows.

"Hush!" said Paolo, putting his ear to the door. "Hush, they're saying something!"

"Both of you knock!" yelled the police chief. "Pound with all your might and tell them to open!"

Now they both began hammering on the door with their fists.

"Stop!" cried Agnolino. "Tell them to open!"

"Open up!"

Agnolino to Pietro: "In the name of the law."

"Yes," said Pietro solemnly.

"You're supposed to call out: 'in the name of the law'!"

"In the name of the law!"

Agnolino hopped on his ancient legs:

"You colossal idiot and cretin! You're supposed to say the whole thing: 'Open up in the name of the law,' dammit!!"

"Open up in the name of the law, dammit!"

Paolo looked disdainfully at him.

"You must shout much louder, *carissimo* colleague!"

"Shout yourself, you coward!"

Paolo in a thundering voice: "Open up in the name of the law!"

The people on the piazza drew back, leaving plenty of space around the two of them. And then the door opened. They retreated a few steps to the side.

"Hush," said Tomaso through the crack in the door, and closed it again.

"Break down the door!" howled Agnolino. "Grab the handle!"

"Not I!" said Pietro. Agnolino flew into a rage, he squeaked and spit:

"Down with the door, I say! Break it down!"

They took hold of the doorknob and jerked it timidly.

"Harder! With all your might! Tear it down!"

Now the door opened for real, and they darted backward. Tomaso's face came into view, and his look was black and terrible, his eyes like slits, and he bared his teeth like a dog.

"You are extremely evil and bad people to disturb us now. What do you want?!"

Agnolino stood alone a good way in front of his troops.

"In the name of the law!" he squeaked. "We want in! Let the police in!"

"I'll beat those two sheep of yours into spaghetti," said Tomaso, pointing at the *carabinieri*. "Those two wretched Sicilians!"

"You Neapolitan!" retorted Paolo scornfully.

"Into pasta!" said Tomaso calmly, and showed with his hands in the air how he would accomplish the task. The two of them now tried to steal away unseen. But Agnolino spotted them.

"Stop!" he shrieked. "In with you!" And then to Tomaso: "You don't dare to close the door on the police! In with you! Will you obey?"

They had come closer, and he went behind them and shoved.

"In with you!"

"*Carissimo* and *reverendissimo* police chief," said Tomaso, "it would never occur to me to do anything so illegal as to bar the door to the police. They can certainly come in, but I have said what we're going to do with them: Spaghetti!"

Pietro and Paolo tried to twist away, but Agnolino wouldn't let go.

"In with you! Hush! Hush! Will you go in?!"

"I've warned you," said Tomaso mildly, but with distorted features. "And there are a little over thirty of us here. But just come in, if you absolutely must!!"

Agnolino foamed and squeaked and pushed, but the two of them resisted, and they were naturally stronger than the old man.

"In, in! Will you obey? In with you, Paolo! In with you, Pietro!"

He struck them.

"You mustn't hit us, *signore*," said Pietro. "It's agains the law."

"I'm not denying entrance to anyone," said Tomaso with flashing eyes, and pushed the door wide open.

"Miserable blockheads!" howled the police chief. "What are you afraid of? After all, you're armed!"

Pietro took a swift step sideways and handed his gun to Agnolino. "Here, dear uncle police chief. You go first!"

"Here is my gun too," said Paolo and handed it to the flabbergasted Agnolino, who stood there with both weapons in his arms.

"It, it, it is your duty to go in first," said he. "Will you immediately take back your guns!"

"Best of all police chiefs! Another time!"

"How in the world did you become *carabinieri*?"

We became *carabinieri* to make a living," said Pietro haughtily, "not a dying. Oh, today the fishermen are extremely stirred up and angry! We'll go in another day."

"You're fired!"

A whisper of quiet indignation went through the crowd. Paolo saw that he had their sympathies on his side, and grew bolder. Maybe too bold. He went too far:

"We are civil servants," he crowed, "and civil servants can't be fired without due process of law. *Fancy that, Edda*!"

Yes, he had gone too far. Agnolino became utterly white with fury, and oddly enough it was the last words which had such an effect on him.

"What!" he foamed, "what did you call me? As if I was Mussolini's daughter! How dare you call me by a girl's name, you most wretched of all your dirty father's many half-witted and neglected children! How dare you call me Edda!"

This frightful outburst terrified Paolo, and he took yet another step backward.

"Most beloved police chief," he said meekly, "I didn't mean anything bad by it. And I certainly didn't mean to say that you were a girl. I would never even hint at such a thing. But it's an expression I've learned from *professore* Anso, he's always saying it: 'Fancy that, Edda!'"[3]

---

3. "Fancy that, Hedda!": a line from Ibsen's *Hedda Gabler* which has become a byword in Norwegian.

Before I could stop him, Arnold had risen from the table and crossed the piazza in a few long strides. Once again his face looked like the French army.

"This is the worst thing I've ever seen!" he said loudly. "I'll go in first! Follow me!"

He swiftly went inside, and with a rapid maneuver Agnolino forced both carabiniers after him, then brought up the rear himself, leaving a bare space outside the trattoria; Tomaso disappeared from the doorway. All was quiet again. No one moved a finger on the piazza. We listened for a moment, then we heard it, coming from inside.

It was a hard, sudden sound like the blow of an axe.

There followed a moment's silence, after which first Paolo, then Pietro and finally Agnolino emerged. No, they were no triumphal procession to be photographed and framed under glass and set beside the Queen of England and Lollobrigida. Agnolino was still carrying the guns, and the door stood open after them. It stood thus for a good while, and then Arnold's form came into view. He was on his legs, but holding his head, and from the slow manner in which he moved it was evident that something tiresome must have happened to him in there. I quietly went over to him and let him lean on me, laying his right arm over my shoulders and grasping him around the wrist with my own right hand. With my left arm around his waist I managed to lead him back to the table. He was utterly silent, like a man who has met resistance. But when he was seated at the table again, he said:

"Oh God, oh!" and clutched his left eye.

It was strange, for now you could see only his right eye, black and swollen. "Oh!" he said.

I ordered him a French cognac. Onto the piazza now came Mayor Lambo and Father Leone, both of whom joined Strozzi and Lippi.

"They're late!" called Lambo to Agnolino. "Something must have happened!"

"Who?" he called back, trying to collect himself.

"The fifty! Shh! They've been delayed. They should have been here by now!"

"Terrible!" quavered Agnolino. "That's most terrible and painful! And the fishermen are highly indignant. They aren't easy to talk to."

He hobbled over and joined the group of the town's fathers. I heard steps beside me, and the tripping of Martin's miniature pinschers. They jumped over Arnold's pantlegs. When I looked up, Martin was standing there.

"My goodness!" he said, "how lovely that I ran into you!"

Arnold groaned, and I looked for Pietro and Paolo, but they were nowhere to be seen. Martin looked aghast at Arnold.

"But goodness gracious! What have you done to yourself, dear friend?"

"Dammit, you can see that I've got a black eye!"

Martin carefully pulled Arnold's hand away from the injured eye.

"Well, for heaven's sakes!" he said, "how idiotic! Has someone been mean to you? No, but my goodness, Arnold! It's completely black and blue! Did you fall on something, my friend?"

Thunderstruck, Martin now took a step backward.

"But Arnold! You actually have *two* black eyes!"

"You don't say," said Arnold bitterly. "You don't say!"

"Yes, you really and truly do! Imagine, two black eyes! Surely something nasty can't have happened to you, can it?"

He drew his pantlegs up carefully and sat down.

"Gosh!" he said, "none of you can tell me what's become of my Georgie-Porgie, can you? There's something I need to talk to him about. Something intimate."

He looked at Arnold and burst into loud, hearty laughter.

"Oh, I'm sorry, Arnold! It's just that you look so *comical* with your two black eyes! But where *is* my Georgie-Porgie? You really haven't seen him, either of you? If only nothing has happened to him! Gosh, he can be so careless, and I'm so worried about him! And now I have to talk to him about something frightfully serious."

"Serious?"

The miniature pinschers jumped and breathed and panted around me. They sniffed at my ankles and licked me. I've never liked them.

"Gracious, yes! Something frightfully serious. Can I confide in you? I'm so *unhappy,* you see!"

"Insofar as I still have my sight intact," said Arnold, "I'd say that you look mighty happy!"

There was reproach in his tone, as if Arnold didn't like the thought that Martin might have solved his social and other problems and become the happier for it.

"Yes, that too," replied Martin, unsuspecting. "Happy, too! Gosh, but it's absolutely to laugh over, if it hadn't been to cry over too. But then I'm both happy and unhappy at once. I'm unhappy mainly for Georg's sake."

"Oh!" said Arnold. "This damned eye!"

"Does your head hurt too?" I said.

"Yes, because you see I don't know how my Georgie-Porgie will take it! If only he doesn't do away with himself when he finds out! He's so sensitive, you know."

"Waiter," called Arnold, "a cognac!" And to Martin: "When he finds out what?"

"Oh, golly, then! Listen, this has to be between us three. But so you understand that I've been at the tailor's. . . ."

Arnold, with a glance at Martin's new pink pants: "Yes, so I see!"

Martin got up and ran his hands down over his hips: "Aren't they just darling?"

"Yes," said Arnold furiously, "simply charming! And so at the tailor's you..."

Martin sat down again. "...spent the whole day, and he took measurements for lots more than just this one pair. I'm getting lots of pants."

"Right," said Arnold. "Then I can well understand that your Georgie-Porgie will be rather unhappy when he gets the bill."

"No," said Martin, blushing slightly, "he's not getting the bill for them. I'm getting them for free. I can get as many pants as I want from him."

"Aha, friendly tailor!" said Arnold.

"Yes," continued Martin, "then he's so charming, you see, and now he's invited me to live with him rent-free, and he's going to make all kinds of clothes for me. He's just so sweeeeet, can you believe it?"

"And Georg?"

"Gracious yes! So it's him I'm thinking of. I just hope he won't be too unhappy, poor thing! If only he doesn't do away with himself!"

"He'll survive, you'll see!" said Arnold.

"You shouldn't take it so lightly!" said Martin. "Georgie-Porgie is actually so sensitive behind all the cynical things he says, and I've been thinking about him the *whole* day!"

"For that matter," I said, "he's been asking after you the *whole* day. But he couldn't find you."

"No, because we were taking my measurements at the tailor's house, in private, that is. Was my Georgie-Porgie unhappy, then?"

"He was drunk."

"That means he was unhappy."

"Then, by God, he's always unhappy!" said Arnold.

Across the piazza, heading for Alexi's, there now came a company consisting of Police Chief Agnolino, Mayor Lambo, *monsignor* Leone, and the two younger gentlemen, hotelkeeper Lippi and tourist chief Strozzi.

"There's no use trying to gain access to the fishermen's meeting," squeaked Agnolino. "They're remarkably agitated."

"And they're late!" wailed Lambo. "Late!"

"Who's late?" growled Leone.

"The fifty. They should have been here by now."

"All right!" said Leone, and looked darkly at the door to the trattoria. "Meanwhile I'll get the fishermen out."

Agnolino jumped in:

"Stop, very best *monsignore*! They are extremely angry!"

Leone laid his heavy hand on the doorknob and opened it with no resistance from inside. He placed himself on the threshold and shouted into the smoky room:

"*Signori pescatori*! Will you do us the great favor of coming out onto the piazza? The mayor has an offer to make you!"

"Don't promise too much!" squeaked Agnolino.

"My good fishermen, be so obliging as to come out to us, so that we can discuss the town's problems under God's open sky!"

"An offer?" called Tomaso from inside.

"Yes, an offer, gentlemen. Come out and then you can hear it!"

"Very well, holy father!" said Tomaso, appearing in the doorway. He turned and shouted to the others: "Come out, everybody! They want to make us an offer!"

"Will they offer us the town treasury?" shouted a fisherman who now appeared in the doorway.

"Probably. Everybody just come out!"

One by one the fishermen came out onto the square. They settled at tables, on steps, on boxes, on the big empty wine barrels beside the door. Many simply remained standing. Agnolino drew Lambo aside and squeaked feebly:

"Perhaps you want to read the riot act for them instead? I myself have got a terrible pain in my throat, best of all friends!"

"It's the police chief's duty," replied Lambo, demurring.

"It's just as much the mayor's!"

"Well!" Tomaso's voice rang over the square. "We're ready to listen to your offer. Be quiet, everybody! We don't want them to trick us!"

He stepped aside and seated himself at the back against the wall of the trattoria, so that he had a view of the whole piazza. There was something about him I didn't like, a strange natural authority, and something crafty, carnivore-like in his eyes. I thought that the scirocco might have been too much for him. So many weeks without regular work, without fishing, and all the time this warm, dead wind from Africa. It was lukewarm on the piazza and I was damp under my collar and on my brow.

"We want the town treasury for our breakwater!" Timberio suddenly shrieked out over the assembly.

"Hush!" said Tomaso.

But more joined in, shouting:

"The town treasury! The town treasury!"

Tomaso rose.

"Yes, but shut your most miserable mouths! We'll get it! One way or another we'll get it!"

It grew quiet again. A dull, dark stillness, a silence which wasn't peace. Something gnashed its teeth and growled at the bottom of it, and I thought how impossible it was for a foreigner to comprehend what really dwelt in these people's souls. It was unknown, a white area on the map.

Agnolino and Lambo were standing just a couple of yards from our table, Leone a bit further away.

"Get out there in the square, best of all friends!" said Lambo, shoving Agnolino ahead of him. "Go out and talk to them! You have the gift for it, *carissimo amico*!"

Agnolino stood there groping in his pockets and finding nothing.

"I don't have the paper with the points! What was it we agreed on?"

"The railway," sighed Lambo.

"And the airships, yes! Now I remember!"

"Materialism!" said Leone.

"But there was more!" squeaked Agnolino desperately. "There was a lot more!"

The fishermen had been waiting for some time, and were getting restive again. You could hear shouts and shrieks. The people were growling.

"The railway, the airships and the very naughty materialism were the most important!" whispered Lambo. "That's enough! Just talk to them! Talk! Talk!"

"We want the treasury!" shouted a fisherman. And more joined him, menacingly: "Yes, the treasury! The treasury! Bring it here!"

Once again Tomaso brought his troops to order; he stood up.

"Of course we'll get the town treasury! Very best, most beloved colleagues and friends! But first, shut up!"

Resolutely Leone pushed the police chief out onto the square, where he stopped and made yet another effort to find his notes. Tomaso waved his hand a couple of times, and two fishermen rolled one of the wine barrels up to the speaker. Then they lifted him carefully onto it. He tottered, but remained standing.

"Don't forget materialism!" said Lambo, who had followed him: "That's the main thing."

"Wait!" said Agnolino, looking down at the other in despair: "I've forgotten the riot act too!"

"Fire away, best, most magnificent friend!" said Lambo and withdrew. Agnolino looked around the hushed, expectant piazza. Then he cleared his throat a couple of times, and raised his feeble voice:

"Citizens of Bellapalma! My dear, grateful people! Already when the railway was brought in, I said…I foresaw what it would bring! I believe today as always that we should never have brought in the railway!"

Murmurs of assent from the people. They nodded their agreement. Agnolino went on:

"It has brought with it, O my dear children of the town, a steadily expanding dissolution of all the good old ways. Children rebel against their parents, parents against grandparents, and…and…."

"…grandparents against great-grandparents!" shouted a fisherman.

"Yes, yes," continued Agnolino in a treble voice, "so it is. This is what has happened. It's highly disgusting to think what unnatural grandparents we have today! They rebel against everything and everybody!

"What then is more natural, my dear, grateful folk, than that the people too should rebel against the God-given authorities!?? People defy their superiors. What has been happening here in Bellapalma today? Rebellion, my children, rebellion! Way back when they brought in the railway I foresaw that it must come. I have always, always, always been against the railway. On this I shall never budge an inch. Alas yes! The time is past when people in Bellapalma lived God-fearing, unassuming, obedient lives, and the generations piously and quietly succeeded one another."

He paused to draw breath, then continued with a steadily more shaky and squeaky voice:

"In the railway's footsteps followed a new and godless time—and selfishness, rebellion, defiance and disaster burst upon Bellapalma, upon our ancient, beloved town. Citizens! It is the *Age* we stand face to face with! The new age, when everything is trampled into ruins, when decency and obedience are at an end. And the old values...."

"What's he talking about?" yelled a fisherman angrily. And he wasn't the only one who had grown impatient. You could hear unrest and conversation, muffled exclamations and snickers all across the square.

"When is he getting to the breakwater?" shouted another. And more joined in the cry: "We want the town treasury!"

Many others simply shouted: "The treasury! The treasury!"

"Hush!" yelled Tomaso. "Let him finish!"

"But the railway," twittered Agnolino, "it thunders forth through the land with smoke and sparks, like—Oh! like the highly evil Devil himself! It scares people and pets up into trees, runs over our cats and seduces our youth! And in the railway's footsteps something else has made its highly devilish entry into Bellapalma! It is mat... mat... You know what I'm thinking of, Lambo! Say it!"

"Materialism!"

"Yes, exactly! Materialism has broken loose in Bellapalma! The train brought not only impudence and disobedience to our little town, but materialism as well. With the train came materialism and..."

"The tourists!" shrieked an angry fisherman. And more joined in eagerly: "Yes, yes, they come by train! Many tourists come by train! *Signor* police chief is absolutely right!"

Agnolino continued:

"Exactly! The tourists and materialism. Materialism, this frightfully loathsome sickness which has come to our little town!"

Agitation and uncertainty reigned among the people, and several times the cry was heard:

"What is materialism? What kind of thing is that?"

There was general bewilderment, and they were all asking each other:

"What is materialism?"

Tomaso rose and demanded silence. Then he whispered:

"You ought to understand that! It is the sickness which Pasquale has caught from the tourists!"

"And a regular pig's sickness it is!" shrieked the old fisherman Giuseppe: "A pig's sickness, I say!"

"And the way it's been spread around!" yelled the red-haired Timberio.

Giuseppe got halfway to his ancient feet and said:

"It's quite right what our best of all police chiefs says; there was practically none of this sickness in the town before the tourists came!"

Not everyone had heard when Tomaso defined materialism for them, and the explanation was now whispered from head to head. All were agreed and indignant over the state of affairs. They supported Agnolino with heart and voice, and nodded to each other.

Agnolino went on:

"Hush! Let me speak, dear children! What we must do is drive materialism back out of our town! Out with this destructive sickness which is laying it waste! Away with it!"

Muffled exclamations: "Yes, yes, out with it!" And a few excited voices whispering: "You hear for yourselves that he says it's a sickness!"

Agnolino further:

"Today materialism encroaches everywhere! But we shall fight it!"

His voice grew steadily stronger from the support he felt around him. He shrieked, he howled, he rolled his eyes, became as high-flown and eloquent as a prince of the Church:

"Cross my heart, fellow citizens! Today it has encroached on us everywhere! We all of us have to some degree been touched by materialism!"

Tomaso thoughtfully:

"That's true! O Madonna, the great majority in this town have had it at least once!"

An agitated fisherman stood up.

"All the waiters have materialism!" he yelled. The fishermen chimed in: "Yes, all of them! The waiters are a bunch of pigs!"

Agnolino with fervent rhetoric:

"Now materialism must be driven out again! We—your police chief, your mayor, your priest, hotelkeeper Lippi and tourist chief Strozzi—have discussed this today. And we have concluded that materialism among the fishermen must now be combatted with the very strongest measures!"

Enthusiastic voices: "Bravo! Bravo!"

A single voice: "Do we get free medicine?"

Agnolino: "And we must deal with it severely! We have found the root of evil, and we will press forward with vigor, now that we are resolved to fight it."

He took a deep breath, turned toward Tomaso, pointed at him and threw himself on the offensive:

"We're especially grieved that you of all people have made yourself a carrier of the contagion! You, Tomaso, who used to be a good and unassuming man, you, *you*! You who were a good fisherman back then when all of you put out to sea every day! You who were—at one time—a good and diligent citizen of Bellapalma, son of good parents, of humble, upright, pious folk— you of all people have long since taken to spreading this around in our beloved, innocent little town!

"That it should be you who are spreading this among our fishermen, that is our greatest sorrow. Look at all those men sitting around you. To them you've brought the contagion! What would your mother have said if she had lived to see it!"

A shriek, a long, mad yowl welled up out of Tomaso. His face was like a tiger, one single wild, contorted grimace. And he got to his feet and pressed forward through the fishermen.

"That's a lie! That's the blackest lie from hell! O Madonna, what a swine of a police chief! That's a very, very ugly lie! In the first place I'm not like that—it's the filthy and monstrously immoral waiters who are like that; and in the second place I haven't had materialism since 1951! And then I got it from a lady—yes, from an English lady who was here for two months and gave materialism to Paolo and Ignazio and Timberio and Caruso! That's a black, a most ugly lie what you're saying, you monstrously filthy toad of a police chief!"

Agnolino stayed on the barrel, swaying as in a strong wind, but he didn't give in. He pointed at Tomaso with his little brown finger and went on:

"*You* are the originator! You are the source of the contagion! Just don't attempt to deny it!"

New roars from Tomaso. He flailed about him and forced his way forward, he created an empty space around him, and with wild, bloodshot eyes he groped for Agnolino. But all was chaos, everybody was shrieking and swarming, and he didn't find him, for the police chief was no longer on the barrel. Up out of all the yells and shrieks on the square rose Tomaso's frenzied voice: "A lie! A lie! That's a black lie!"

The disorder was total, and the sea of people billowed like a real ocean around the table where we were sitting. Again we heard Tomaso's roar:

"And to say such a thing about me! When everybody knows what Pasquale and Augusto have been cooking up with their materialism!"

For a while it billowed back and forth, and gradually the storm abated. Tomaso was quiet, and I saw him lean feebly, almost exhausted, against the wall of the trattoria. He no longer looked normal, and was breathing heavily, with his whole chest and belly. Then Father Leone's splendid bass rang over the piazza. We looked up, and on Agnolino's abandoned wine barrel towered the prelate's beefy body.

"Hush!" he said. "Silence!"

And you could have heard a pin drop. Everyone listened. And through the silence a fisherman said: "We want the town treasury to build the breakwater with!"

"That's right," answered the man of God, "you shall have it!"

Father Leone's very first words already proclaimed the great evangelist and preacher. Oh, how we were convicted in our sin at the sight of him! A puritan majesty flamed up from the figure who stood on the wine barrel. The people waited obediently, expecting some terrible condition for getting the money. But it didn't come. Instead Leone continued:

"You shall get the money to build the breakwater! It is truly a very long time since I've heard anything which has pleased me so exceedingly much as the report that you want to get to work and build a harbor. I am wholeheartedly on your side in this question; you shall get the town treasury!"

Now the rejoicing broke loose. The fishermen stood and shrieked, shouted, threw hats and loose objects into the air: "*Monsignor* is on our side! Hurrah! Hurrah! He is truly an extremely good person! Bravo! Bravo! He's on our side!"

And much else.

Leone, continuing: "This very day, this evening you shall get the treasury, if you wish!"

New rejoicing, new shouts: "O Madonna, no, not this evening! That is too much! That is too wild! Bravo! Bravo! Tomorrow is soon enough!"

Thus did the people rejoice.

On the other hand the flame of enthusiasm was weak in Agnolino and Lambo, who, together with Lippi and Strozzi, were standing beside our table.

"Now surely he's going too far!" said Lambo cautiously.

"Imagine, without consulting the temporal authorities!" police chief Agnolino whispered back, his white moustache aquiver.

"He's speaking with forked tongue!" Lippi whispered to them.

A tiger's roar from Tomaso filled the square: "Hush! Absolute silence! If anyone disturbs *monsignor* in his most excellent speech, then I'll knock him as flat as a very little, terribly repulsive louse! Only *monsignor* is to speak! No one must interrupt him!"

"Yes, quiet!" called several fishermen.

"Long," continued Leone, "long have I yearned to hear such a resolution from you fishermen. For I will no longer conceal the fact, no, I will no longer keep it a secret that I have looked with the very deepest sorrow on developments in Bellapalma in recent years. *O buonissimi pescatori!* The very, very deepest sorrow!"

Voices from the people: "Yes! Hear! Hear! He's right! *Monsignor* is grieved!" Etc.

Leone: "The tourist trade has brought a false and harmful prosperity to us all. A highly false wealth! Who can't eat his fill in Bellapalma today? Who can't dress well? You walk on the beach and on the square in fine clothes, watch television in the bars and drink espresso and anisette all day long! All are well-fed! All have clothes!"

Voices: "Yes, that's right! All have money and food!"

"But what has the town not paid for this affluence? For this world's glittering gold and false jewels! Ha! What price haven't we paid? Have you really done honest work for this wealth? No!

"You have bought it at a terrible price!"

A hush in the crowd.

Leone: "Do you maybe go out and fish anymore? As good as never! Only once in a while when you get too bored with playing cards at Alexi's or sitting on the beach. In the summer you sit on the beach and rent out your boats to the swimming guests, and pose for photographs—or row the tourists around—and for this you earn more money than you could earn by honest fishing. Is this a life for sons of the sea? For the trueborn fishermen of

Bellapalma? Oh, no, no! It is a lazy man's life which demoralizes! Which destroys."

Scattered shouts: "Yes, that's true! He's right!"

"And I know of things which are worse! I have heard that many of the fishermen reap material benefits from certain foreign ladies who come here! That many receive the support of ladies from many lands!"

"Yes," said a fisherman happily, "many of these foreign ladies are extremely nice. They buy us fishing nets and tackle."

"I have heard," said Father Leone, "that many fishermen maintain connections with up to several nice ladies at once. Is this true, Tomaso?"

Tomaso looked down and to the side.

"Very best, *carissimo monsignore*! The kind ladies come from the countries by the northern seas, and the men in those lands have exceedingly thin and bad blood. Those men have blood which is no warmer than the water in the North Sea. Many of these ladies have made us gifts of fishing nets and tackle and other things which fishermen may need. And holy father, it goes without saying that the more ladies you receive support from, the more money you make in the course of a year."

"Does this apply to you too, Tomaso?"

"Oh, holy father, must I answer this exceedingly difficult question?"

"How many ladies do you receive support money from?"

"O *signore*! From four ladies, one from Holland, one from England and…."

"Thank you, Tomaso. That is sufficient. Such things are a shame!"

"But what are we to do, father?"

"You shall fish," said Leone forcefully, "fish! Now things are going to be different, once you get the breakwater and the harbor!"

"Won't the ladies come anymore then?" called a young fishermen.

Leone, enthusiastically: "No, then there will be an end to the lusts of the flesh! How many of you have the kind of female contributors that *signor* Tomaso has? The kind that buy nets and tackle? Stand up, all those who have generous acquaintances!"

Amid muttering and stifled protests the fishermen stood up. It took some time, and gradually one man became the object of the whole piazza's attention. All thoughts were directed to one single man. People craned their necks, shoved others aside, stood on tiptoe to see. It was old man Vittorio, who had remained seated.

"Shame on you!" cried Leone harshly. "Is Vittorio the only pious person among you?"

Timberio, the red-haired giant, seized the floor:

"Holy father, *O reverendissimo monsignore*! Our colleague Vittorio, the *grandissimo pescator*, is an exceedingly aged gentleman! He will be eighty-seven years old in the month of April! May he live many, many more years among us!"

Many: "Yes, *monsignore*! That is our heartfelt wish!"

"Hush!" roared Leone. "Hush! Most people have their full powers even at that age, and misuse them dreadfully!"

The people chimed in, and one heard the name of Police Chief Agnolino mentioned repeatedly.

"Hush!" said Leone. "Now sit down, my children!"

They sat down, relieved that the interrogation was over. Leone again took the floor:

"But now there will be an end to this! And I've rejoiced inwardly that the decision to build the breakwater comes from you, my good fishermen! You shall once more become honest seamen, practice your holy, simple fisherman's work again, just as your fathers did before you!

"Nothing in recent years has pleased me so much as that you have now made this decision—to go back to your true work again! You shall regain your old dignity and pride. You shall brave all kinds of weather! When the breakwater goes up, then you can put out to sea every single day, in any weather, and live off the hard and worthy toil of your own hands!"

Timberio now swallowed all shame and posed his question as he stood up:

"Very best *monsignore,* must we also fish when it's raining?"

Leone: "Naturally! After all, you're fishermen! Of course you must also go fishing in rainy weather. That's when the fish bite best! Oh, they have a hearty *appetito* when it's raining!"

Another fisherman said: "But there are exceedingly few fish in the sea!"

"My children!" said Leone, "then you must venture further out on the ocean. You must find the fish where they are! Seek them out, find their secret hiding places, catch them from a hundred fathoms deep! Oh, you shall become true fishermen again! When the breakwater comes, you'll have a really good harbor here. It will never again be impossible to get your boats through the surf, you will no longer need to drag them up on the beach to protect them from the ocean's raging waves! In the future you will fish both day and night, in storm and rain, in the treacherous *mezzogiorno* and *scirocco,* as well as in the cold *maestrale*! In all kinds of weather!"

"Do we have to go out in a high wind too?" called a fisherman.

"Of course! That's what they did in the old days!"

"But that's dangerous! It's exceedingly dangerous!"

"Everything is in God's hands! Trust in Him, just as your ancestors did!"

"*Monsignore*! Must we also go out in the biting west wind?"

"Yes, *signor pescatore*! Far out on the ocean! Far, far out!"

A whispering voice: "I don't want to do that!"

Others: "Me neither! Not on my life!"

"Hush!" shrieked Leone, waxing wroth: "What kind of effeminate nonsense is that? If the community builds the breakwater for you, then of course you will please fish! You will go out! Out with you! You shall become regular, honest fishermen again! Oh, the town will again be extremely proud of its sons! Now there will be an end to French and English and Dutch and Danish ladies—now there will be *work* done here!"

"Why can't the nice ladies come?" called someone.

"Oh, children!" said Leone with a happy sigh from his huge chest. "If you knew how I'm gladdened by the thought of your returning to your forefathers' stern and harsh life, a life without idleness and sloth and tips!"

Another voice: "Won't the very kind ladies come in the spring?"

Leone: "No, never again! Praise be! When the breakwater is built, then there will no longer be any bathing beach, no naked legs and backs, the tourists will be gone for good, the hotels and restaurants will close, and everything will be like it was in the old days. Of course there'll be no more ladies. Life will be harsh and poor, the waiters too will have to become fishermen if they want to live in this town—and you must all revert to the life of your forefathers. You shall fish! In poverty and struggle—but in virtue. Yes, in virtue and poverty!"

"But there are so few fish in the sea!"

"So find them, I said! You must be on the sea day and night, in rain and wind and cold, in storm and in waves; then the catch will surely get better! Far, far out on the sea, where the best and fattest fish dwell in their caves on the ocean floor! If you don't find fish by the coast, where you yourselves have helped kill them off with dynamite, then look for them in the ocean!"

A heavy, painful silence settled over the piazza. Heads sank, light went out of eyes, the happy smiles vanished. A lone voice sounded:

"Not on my life will I go out so far! It's against progress!"

"Listen!" said Leone sternly. "This is serious. We're beginning another life in Bellapalma from this hour. You can, as I said already, get the town treasury today. You've already made your choice. Tomorrow begins the building of the harbor!"

"Aren't the extremely kind ladies coming this year?" said Timberio.

"Never again! No more tourists! That's finished."

"Yes, but my lady has promised me a motor for my boat."

"When we have the breakwater, then you can row!"

"I'd rather have a motor!"

Pandemonium broke loose, and it turned out that many had claims to pursue.

"Quiet!" yelled Leone angrily. "From now on it will be as in the old days. I won't tolerate contradictions now! None! And neither will Tomaso! We'll have it like in the old days, poor and harsh, but virtuous and good! —Oh, *signore* Vittorio, you excellent fisherman! You remember the good old days. Rise, ancient witness, and tell us about the old, true, unspoiled Bellapalma! Tell of the olden days' piety and pure living!"

Vittorio rose willingly, and all eyes followed him.

"O Madonna," he said, "it is so true, so true what *monsignor* says! It was a life for strong people. It was very, very bad to live here in the old days! Only the hardest and toughest and strongest could make it!"

"That's right," said Leone kindly, "tell us how people endured a life of danger and privation here in Bellapalma before the tourists came!"

Vittorio sank down for a moment into his own remembered images, then fetched them up for us and went on:

"Yes, it was very hard! Many died on the sea and left widows and children behind. I remember the time when we forbade fathers and sons to go to sea in the same boat, so that two men in the same family wouldn't die if the boat was lost. When we didn't catch any fish, then there was hunger. Oh, many were very, very hungry! And we hardly ever ate the fish ourselves when we caught any, for they were too costly for that. No one could afford to eat fish. And besides we had nowhere to cook them back then, and wood and charcoal were too expensive to buy. No, most people had nothing to cook on. We ate almost nothing but bread back then. Yes, that was a harsh time!"

He looked down into himself again for a little while, and no one spoke. Then he continued:

"It was then the great emigration began. Oh yes! It wasn't easy to be here, no."

His voice trembled a bit and he fell silent at the memories.

"Yes, but a pious time?" asked Leone gently. "With good, strict morals and a godfearing life?"

"Oh, yes!" replied Vittorio with a faint smile, "that's true! The worse the fishing was, the more devout people became. We were always going to church to pray for better fishing, but it wasn't always much help, for it was in those years that the fish disappeared. And the old *monsignore*, the holy father who was here before Father Leone, we always asked him to come down to the beach and bless the boats and the tackle before we put out, and the catch would surely have been even worse if he hadn't helped us."

"Those were hard times, all right!" said Father Leone, "but with strict morals and a devout life, where people cherished the old values. People were surely happier back then."

Vittorio smiled faintly and slowly shook his head.

"Oh no," he said quietly, "they certainly weren't happier. But it's true that we were very devout and that we were zealous at praying in church. And materialism, that we almost never had! And it was good that it was so rare, for it was a much more difficult disease to cure back then, and none of us could afford to go to the doctor— and besides, there weren't any doctors living in Bellapalma at that time. We were much too poor for any doctor to make a living here. Yes, people died of it if they got that disease. Like Gatini's Giovanni, although Giovanni was a very young boy. Well, I'm probably the only one here who remembers."

He fell silent now, and just stood looking at the pictures inside himself, then he raised his head and said in a faint voice:

"There weren't many people to be seen in the streets back then, and it was very rare to see anyone with shoes on. Today we all wear shoes, and take them off only when we go in the boat. No, I don't believe we were happier, *monsignore*. And when all the people were hungry, then what happened was that people went away; either they went to other towns where there was work to be had, or they journeyed all the way to America. Yes, most of them went to a town over there called Brooklyn. I know many who journeyed very, very far away from Bellapalma."

One of the fisherman rose halfway and said heavily:

"Yes, that's true! Many people left because there was so little food here back then!"

Vittorio looked at him as if reminded of something forgotten.

"It was in that time that the whole upper city was left standing empty because people went away. All the houses in that part of town which we call *Cità morte* to this very day, were left empty, and you could see dead houses all over, and all of Bellapalma became an extremely quiet town. There were few people to be seen in the streets, for of course there's no land to till here by the coast, and the fishing had become extremely bad—Excuse me, *signori*, but it makes me sad to think of it!"

"Don't you remember a few more things from the good old times?" said Father Leone carefully.

"Oh yes, I remember one thing and another!" replied the fisherman as he stood looking down, "and many people whose names no one here knows, and I remember what happened to them. People often went about dressed in rags, and if it got a bit cold in the winter they really froze, for we had nothing to heat with. And many got sick from the bad food or because they didn't have any food, and if they couldn't manage to go fishing because they had fever, then things got even worse for everybody. And the children weren't well off either. And then there was the disease called tuberculosis which came here and took many away. And it was hard to get help, for we had neither the motor road nor this, this railway back then. No, no, that we didn't have."

"And then the tourists came?" said Leone.

"Yes, yes, then the tourists gradually came, yes. And then everything changed. Then it got the way it is today. And everybody knows how that is."

He looked around, and many nodded. The fisherman who had spoken once before said half aloud that it was just as Vittorio had said. For his own father had also told about that, and that's exactly how it was!

"You can sit down again," said Father Leone gently to Vittorio, and then he turned to all the people on the square.

"And so now you won't put up with the waiters and the tourists anymore? Now there will be and end to that! You want to be fishermen and go back to just fishing? Live by fishing alone? Build the harbor and the breakwater?"

There was no triumph, no irony in Leone's voice as he looked out over the piazza, over all the bowed heads, the dimmed faces. There was almost no protest from the people sitting there, only a subdued mumbling, a few shaking their heads. But it was all over. A still, three-thousand-year-old sadness lay over the square. Tomaso too sat still and sunken into himself. Then Timberio rose with bowed head.

"No," he said, "we don't want any breakwater after all."

No one protested, they just nodded weakly. And a few stood up, crestfallen, perplexed, as if they had nowhere to go from here.

"Wait a bit, children!" cried Leone. "Listen!"

"There's no use going off with your tails between your legs. Our good friend hotelkeeper Lippi has a few words to say to you after me. But first let me tell you that you fishermen are the town's trueborn children, you are still Bellapalma's pride and joy! Without you we couldn't call ourselves 'a real fishing village on the Mediterranean!' How could we make such a claim? What would Strozzi and the others put on the travel posters without you? Could we maybe paint fishing boats on the posters? Oh, no! My good fishermen, without you there would be no question of writing 'genuine folk life' on these posters which are so important to our town. It's precisely because Bellapalma is a wholly natural, unspoiled little fishing village that the tourists come here! You are the town's most beloved sons, and so long as you have your boats, lovely and yellow and red down on the beach, the tourists will come here! And as you know yourselves, many of the foreigners come to Bellapalma just because of you! Let no one cast the first stone when someone sacrifices himself to the tourist trade, and thus brings life and prosperity to the whole town, *signori pescatori!*"

"Yes," shouted one of the fishermen, "that's true! We are still the ones who feed Bellapalma!"

"But the town hasn't always thought enough of you!" continued Leone, "and it has certainly not always shown you enough appreciation! Therefore our good friend Signor Lippi will now say a few words to you, and make you a small offer!"

Father Leone now, with dignity but sure and light-footed, climbed down off the wine barrel. At the same time a clear disquiet went through the crowd, and it found a vent in the words:

"We don't want the town treasury!"

"Dear sons of the town!" said Lippi, who had taken over Father Leone's pulpit, "Fear not! You shall be spared the town treasury! You shall be spared the breakwater!—You shall be remembered with something quite different!"

He lifted the tambourine which no one had noticed, and beat a quick flourish on it. It went like a whiplash through the crowd, and no one resisted the wild, Arabic rhythm of the instrument. All knees, spinal columns, necks yielded to the desire to follow the rhythm; then he stopped and raised the tambourine above his head, where he held it with outstretched arm and merely jingled it.

"Everybody!" he yelled. "Today you are all my guests for as much wine as it may be your pleasure and joy to drink! I believe that every hotelkeeper in Bellapalma will join me in this!"

A momentary hush, then a burst of applause and shouting:

"Bravo! Bravo!"

Lippi paused and lowered his big, glad eyes to the piazza; all quieted down and followed the hotelkeeper's gaze. Under him, beside the barrel, Father Leone was preparing his famous trick which everyone had heard of, but almost nobody had seen. With a faint, almost embarrassed and happy smile he grasped the back of a chair with his left hand and began stroking the seat with his right. His big hand glided back and forth over the thin plywood, and it looked as if he were caressing it; his hand moved with calm, massaging motions—and then something happened of which I've never in my life heard or seen the like: Under this amazing massage there arose a swirl of rhythms; a devil-may-care, mad dance rhythm, so loud and resonant that it must have been heard all over town. It eddied through heads and senses like a shot, and everyone recognized the tune that he was playing. A couple of loud voices sang the words, and two fishermen, hand in hand, threw themselves into a tango-like, pantomimic dance. More joined in. For a moment all was laughter and song. Then it stopped abruptly. The swirls which for a little while had been almost visible in the air collapsed like an empty sack and sank to earth.

A thin child's voice sounded over the piazza and everyone listened. The boy Benjamino came all the way up to the barrel.

"Strozzi!" he cried. "Strozzi!"

"Yes," said Strozzi, stepping into the limelight for the first time that evening, "what is it, my boy?"

"O Madonna!" yelled Benjamino at the sight of him. "A whole busload of tourists has arrived, just opposite the Piazza del Sole! There are masses of people and no one there is to greet them!"

Strozzi drew himself up and shouted:

"They're here! They're here! Everybody up to welcome them! There are more than fifty of them! Up to the piazza, now, and show a little genuine folk life! First and foremost the *signori* fishermen! It'll be a big surprise for everybody to see what kind of tourists they are!"

He flailed with his arms, and the square was quickly emptied of people. They were like a river, which contrary to nature ran out of the piazza and uphill; the stream of people flowed up streets and stairs toward the Piazza del Sole.

Only Arnold, Martin, and I remained in the dark, warm evening.

"Gracious, but I don't understand a thing of all this!" said Martin. "But now I *must* find my Georgie-Porgie!"

He stood up.

"Good luck!" said Arnold.

Me, I said nothing, for during the last part of the scene I'd been trying to keep an eye on Tomaso. But I couldn't see him anywhere, and I was anxious about him. Besides I had The Girl to think about, and began nursing a faint hope that she would come back this evening.

But just as Martin left, a voice sounded from the edge of the square:

"Arnold! Oh, Arnold!"

It was Kari; she came over to the table breathless and upset.

"Oh, finally, Arnold!" she said. "Thank God I found you! Believe me, I've had a terrible experience!"

She put her arms around his neck.

"You and me, Arnold! But now I'm here, and I'll never leave you again!"

"What?" said Arnold, and lifted his wounded head.

"Now I've come to you, to my Arnold!"

She put two books on the table.

"This is all I own in this world! All I could manage to take with me! Everything else I had to leave there—all my baggage, everything! Oh, Arnold!"

Again she put her arms around his neck and squeezed.

"What's happened?" he groaned, half-smothered.

"Now I've come to you, Arnold! Now you'll never be lonely again! And I did manage to bring away these two books. Oh, Arnold, I've come to stay!"

"Can't you try to say what's happened?"

"Gosh, yes! I couldn't pay the rent, you see! So now I'm homeless and all alone in the world. Now that I've come to you for good, it no longer matters so much that I can't go on living in Bellapalma, for now we can go together to France and live in a nice little town there! Oh, you and me, Arnold!"

She must have been holding him a little too tightly around the neck, for when he had got free he had a hard time speaking; he had to clear his throat and stretch his neck several times.

"That was really nice!" he said hoarsely and softly. "That was… hm…really nice. And what are those books you have with you? I didn't know you were *that* interested in literature, that you'd save books and let the other stuff be!"

He reached out and picked up the books from the table.

"I can't live without them!" said Kari. Arnold now read the titles.

"Hm," said he. "Dale Carnegie: *How to Win Friends and Influence People*, and good old Van der Velde: *Ideal Marriage*....Yes, that's some library!"

He looked up and smiled. Yes, Arnold smiled! He put his hand to his newest and sorest eye and smiled painfully.

"Perhaps we should go home and read a little?" he said.

Kari jumped for joy, but stopped and exclaimed anxiously:

"But Arnold! You've got another one!"

I got up and took my leave.

The Piazza del Sole was brightly lit, and full of people—especially fishermen and waiters, but others had gathered as well. The year's first tourists were arriving, and the mood was like a village in Western Norway when there are rumors that herring are shoaling in the fjord. People came running and singing from all sides, comforted and expectant. Strozzi quickly climbed on a table and spoke:

"Citizens, O most beloved children! Today marks the year's first major influx of foreigners to our town! I will not yet reveal what kind of foreigners they are, but there are fifty of them, and they will be very nice to associate with! Just wait here a minute! Everybody wait, and when I come back we'll sing the town's ancient, highly glorious song! Our very dearest friend, Lippi, will play his tambourine!"

He hopped down off the table and Lippi climbed up.

"Everybody ready? Now let's sing...!"

He raised his voice and led off at a high pitch, but nobody followed him, for Strozzi had returned sooner than expected, and he wasn't alone. The space around, behind and in front of him swarmed, foamed, and seethed with girls. A whole river of girls was flowing into the Piazza del Sole. And they were all blonde. There were dyed blondes and bleached blondes, there were golden blondes, ash blondes and white blondes, there were shampoo blondes and hydrogen peroxide blondes. It was a world of blondies.

"Here come our guests!" yelled Strozzi. "Look!"

A deep growl of pleasure went through the band of fishermen and waiters. It was like the feeding-growl in the lion cage at a zoo when the meat is passed out. The girls looked happy and cheerful, and seemed prepared for the worst.

"These are our honored guests!" shouted Strozzi. "They are fifty young French career women, all from the highly excellent city of Marseilles! Welcome to our little town, and join in the little fiesta we're celebrating today for the town saint, for St. Bobbo, Bellapalma's protector! In our town only friendship reigns, and peace and joy and unity."

Lippi grabbed the tambourine, and the people sang and danced. A couple of wine barrels were rolled onto the piazza, and the waiters came laden with wicker bottles. The noise was intense.

Beside me stood Cesare, the old vagrant.

"*Buonissimo professore,*" he said, "*sempre avanti!*"

"Ever onward, very best Cesare!" I replied. "Life is hard, *amico*!"

"O Madonna, *signore*, exceedingly hard!"

"Our good friend Strozzi didn't mention to us what profession these certainly very nice ladies from Marseilles practice," I said. "Can you, O *eccelentissimo* Cesare, give me a hint?"

"O Madonna!" he said mildly, "it is a very old profession!"

We stood silent a little while. Then Cesare spoke:

"O most excellent *professore*! Perhaps we ought to enjoy a glass of wine together and not worry about something that doesn't concern us personally! Materialism is still a fact in Bellapalma!"

"Cesare, you best of all vagrants, yes, let's enjoy a glass!"

"You are a wise man, *professore*, and it is very smart of you to drink wine now before night falls and people are going to sleep."

We had found a bar, and raised our glasses.

"*Salute*, and *sempre avanti*!"

"*Salute*, and *sempre avanti*!"

He stroked his forehead with the back of his wrinkled brown hand and looked up at the starry sky over the piazza.

"*Professore*, the weather is changing. Tomorrow we'll have the *maestrale*."

A little later I mounted the barrel and sang for the people. First I chose "Paul his chickens," and since the acclaim was like a hurricane, I sang an encore, namely "The old woman with the cane."

Amid resounding applause I clambered down and turned to the owner of one of Bellapalma's many trattorias.

"How did you like my singing, very best *signor* Angelo?" I asked, fishing for praise.

"O Madonna, *professore!* The song was *bellissimo!* Extremely *bellissimo!* I count it as one of the loveliest songs I have heard!"

"And my voice," said I, "did you also enjoy the singing itself?"

"Very best *professore!* The only thing which surpassed the song was the voice that sang it! It was exceedingly lovely! La Scala in Milano is also *bellissima!* In former years I have heard Benjamino Gigli sing there. He too had a *veramente* most lovely voice. Tenor, just like *professore* himself."

Someone took me by the arm. It was young Matteo.

"*Professore!*"

"Yes, Matteo, you detestable boy!"

"*Professore,* you must come! There's something the matter with Tomaso! He's become so strange and is shouting that he wants to bring back Vittorio Emanuele and restore the monarchy in Italy, and besides he's insulted one of the foreign gentlemen. Oh, he's insulted him very, very badly!"

"Matteo, I'm coming! Show me the way!"

"He's at Alexi's, *professore!*"

We set off at a run.

In the midst of the crowd in front of the trattoria was an open space. There Arnold and Kari sat at the table, and Martin stood beside them. The pink, eel-slim pants gleamed in the dark, and he had tethered the miniature pinschers to a table leg. Farther off stood Tomaso, baring his teeth. He had an anisette bottle in his hand and was talking loudly and contemptuously, wildly sawing the air. Scirocco, madness and liquor shone from him. He gesticulated at Martin and yelled:

"Ha, a very evil and bad foreigner! Nobody knows if he's a boy or a girl! You are truly a very great shame to your mother!"

Martin had a sweater over his shoulders, and was otherwise wearing only a shirt and pants. His whole body shook and his cheeks turned white and red. The fine, silky blond hair hung down over his face. A couple of onlookers laughed, but most were silent. Arnold sat at the table looking down. He had been put out of commission.

I went over to Tomaso and took him by the arm, and he looked at me with eyes which hardly recognized me. They were bloodshot and narrowed under the drawn, black eyebrows.

"Another time, *professore!*" he said darkly. Then he raised his head and sent a new stream of insults and swearwords over Martin.

"Tomaso!" I said, grabbing him again by the arm, "let the boy be, now. He hasn't done anything to you, and he's a friend of mine!"

Heedless, he pushed me away with his elbow as he raised the bottle to his lips. There was nothing I could do about that elbow. It was hard and firm as a tree trunk.

"It's best that you go," I said to Martin.

"No!" said Martin, trembling: "I'm not going!"

Tomaso took the bottle from his mouth and continued his derision of Martin, but it had no effect. Martin stood there. After a few more attempts, Tomaso tried another tactic, and singled out Kari.

"Oh," he said, "there sits an evil and extremely wretched woman! I have seen her with all the foreigners who have been in Bellapalma! I won't take in my mouth what kind of woman she is!"

Kari shrieked like a knife-jab, grabbed Arnold by the arm, and set up a wail. Unfortunately Tomaso now began to take in his mouth precisely what kind of woman he thought Kari was, and he did it thoroughly and in detail. Only when he paused for breath between insults could you hear her weeping. Otherwise a deep silence reigned on the square.

"Tomaso," I said, "now you must get hold of yourself!"

Arnold sat quite still, red in the face, looking down. After the day's foray into politics he was a broken man; he was in no condition to do anything.

Then all at once something totally different happened. Martin, who had put up with humiliations and insults on his own account, now became another person.

"I won't tolerate listening to him speak like that to a lady!" he said.

"No," I said, "take her away, and I'll stay here with Tomaso."

Then Martin's high, light voice rang across the piazza:

"Shut up! You disgusting, vulgar scum!"

This is what Tomaso had wanted; he set the bottle down on a table and walked with slow, rocking movements over toward Martin. There was a sigh from the crowd.

"Run!" I said. "Run like the devil!"

"Not on your life," said Martin, white in the face. "Now this vile scum is going to get a licking!"

He slung his pullover on the table and took off his tie. Then he rubbed the palms of his hands together.

"You foul turd!" he said to Tomaso. "You uncultured scum!"

Tomaso had almost reached him, and I had to summon all my courage to place myself between them. Tomaso wasn't in his right mind, and he swept me away with his forearm. People were leaving now, they didn't want to watch the loathsome thing that was about to happen.

"Come on, Arnold!" I said, "We must prevent this!" But Arnold sat as if nailed to his chair. Mute and pale.

I looked at Tomaso and Martin. The one dark and broad as a door, with huge brown hands. And the other thin and slender and pink, trembling and quaking. There was no denying that Martin was of uncommonly elegant build, unbelievably slim over the hips, with delicate wrists and long, slender hands. It was he who struck first, with the flat of his hand and over Tomaso's ear.

Then Tomaso struck, and it whistled in the air. But in the air. He struck yet again, and had the air been an opponent, it would have been defeated. Now ensued a remarkable scene; Tomaso chased Martin around the square, striking out again and again, but without connecting. Oh, he got in a couple of hits, but they were more grazes than punches. Only a very few times did Martin strike back, and it didn't look as if there was any weight in the blows. But they were fast and precise, and made a good bang. In the midst of all this you could hear Tomaso breathing. A peculiarity of the fight was that time after time Martin saved himself by a kind of strange leap—a long spring to the side. I had never before seen anyone jump like that; he sprang several yards at a time. All the same it was ominous, for sooner or later Tomaso must get hold of him on the little piazza, and what happened then would be unpleasant to witness.

The fight was divided into three phases.

First Martin was chased for several minutes, during which Tomaso grew warm and breathless, while Martin showed not a trace of strain. Then came the next phase, where Martin hit back more and more often. In mid-flight he would stop and strike, in the solar plexus, over the ears, around the neck, and then he was gone again. After this phase Tomaso was breathing like a steam engine, and you could hear his heart pounding. Things looked bad. And we noticed that his punches, still landing in the air, were getting slower and slower. Eventually they were more like flapping and waving than true blows.

When the third phase began, it was clear that the tide had turned. Martin too was winded now, dark red in the face and sweating slightly, but he was just as light on his feet as in the beginning, just as lightning-quick, and his punches had if anything gotten heavier and surer. What happened next was that Tomaso got a licking. He got a thorough licking, calm and systematic: from all sides, from before and behind, from below and above the blows rained on him. But he could take a lot, and it cost Martin hard and sustained physical exertion before Tomaso sank to his knees on the piazza and hid his face in his hands, barely able to keep his balance. Then Martin stopped hitting him and came to a standstill beside him. In a quiet, almost friendly tone he asked:

"Have you discovered whether I'm a boy or a girl?"

Tomaso could hardly talk for panting and exhaustion, but he managed to get out the words:

"O Madonna! You are in truth very much a boy, *signore!*"

"Will you ask the young lady's pardon for insulting her?"

Pause. Then, with great emphasis and unction:

"O *signora!* I regret most dreadfully that the evil in me got the upper hand! I regret it most strongly and terribly!"

Martin came over to the table and put on his tie again. He laid the sweater around his shoulders and patted the dogs, who jumped up on his pantlegs.

"Oh, gracious!" he said. "What poor little doggie-woggies! Did pappa forget all about you? Oh, pappa has been naughty to his precious little doggies!"

Arnold stared at him through his battered eyes.

"How..." said he, "how was it possible?"

Martin straightened up and let the doggies jump as much as they wanted. He took out a pocket comb and combed his hair.

"What?" he said. Arnold just stared.

Me, I was feeling superior in a totally different way; for during the last act of Tomaso's tragedy on the piazza I had grasped the truth.

"But it's completely natural!" I said to Arnold. "It was all a matter of course! Don't you understand?"

Kari had dried her tears long since, and was now eating Martin with big blue eyes. Arnold didn't exist for her, and I knew that wherever she ended up sleeping tonight, she would dream of Martin.

"No," said Arnold, "I just don't get it!"

"Dear heart!" I said, "it's as easy as pie! The explanation is right under your nose. And you're supposed to be a best-selling writer in French! In such a difficult language!"

He looked at me, meek and questioning.

"No," he said, "explain it to me, please!"

There was no doubt that Arnold was on the way to becoming a new person, so to speak a writer with deeper interests.

"Arnold," I said, "listen!"

And he listened.

It was when the fight was entering its third and last phase that I had hit on the explanation of Martin's remarkable speed and strength. The thing is that Martin, despite his youth, is one of the best ballet dancers in his hometown, and this hometown is a large city with a world-famous ballet. It was Martin's job to practice classical ballet six hours a day, which he'd been doing for at least six or seven years. I let Arnold in on my train of thought.

"So you must imagine what kind of conditioning he gets from it!" I said. "It's his work to do knee bends on one leg with a grown woman on an arm stretched straight over his head. That's a bit different from sitting and scratching at a typewriter!"

The question marks in Arnold's eyes went out.

"Of course," he said, "that explains everything. That means that Martin could probably have licked a couple more Tomasos besides, once he got going?"

"Sure," I said expansively. "Martin is probably a little stronger than the average circus artist."

⁋⁌

Martin had risen, and we both looked fondly and admiringly at him. I'd never been so at one with Arnold before; we were at bottom very good friends now. The knuckles on Martin's slender, smooth hands were red and rather the worse for wear. He himself didn't look happy.

"Mercy me!" he said anxiously. "I don't understand where my Georgie-Porgie has got to! Can't you help me look for him?"

As if on command, we both got to our feet.

"Yes, you bet we want to help you! You'd better believe that we'll join the search!"

Alas, we didn't find Georg that night, though we kept at it until one in the morning. And Bellapalma was hardly the right place to conduct searches in; a town where all the inhabitants are using their collective energy to drink wine, sing arias, play guitar, beat on tambourines, dance with peroxide blondes. or purely and simply stand on piazzas and stairs and howl at the stars—such a town does not have the gravity needed to find a missing friend.

Me, I was rather distracted by thoughts of The Girl and when she would come back to Bellapalma. Thus we lacked all the prerequisites for organizing a really serious search party to find the missing Georg. He was and remained lost.

SEVEN

Early the next morning I went up through the streets to the Sunshine Bar. The sun was shining and the sea was imperturbably blue, but still everything was different. The air was fresh and cool, a healthy, natural winter morning, with cold shadows and pleasant warmth in the sun. It was lovely to be wearing a sweater. On the beach many of the fishing boats had already been shoved out, and others were being put in the water as I walked past. Everyone said hello and smiled. There was an end to scirocco and crisis and nerves, the sea was shiny in toward shore, but with a slight rippling further out. Along the beach the wind was calm.

High up over Bellapalma, over the clear mountaintops more than six thousand feet up, another wind was blowing: the mistral, the cold, chaste north wind which makes people healthy and life natural. Bellapalma is never reached directly by the mistral, the town lies too well hidden in a hollow under the mountains. The cold in the wind never gets to us, just the coolness, the freshness reaches down to us in our sunny hollow. We lie in the lee of the mistral itself, but enjoy its benefits.

For dinner there would be fresh fish at Alexi's. No surf, no need for a breakwater, full opportunity for the boldest to catch a few pounds. Life took its course, the sun climbed its golden track and all nature functioned splendidly. I still had my back pocket crammed full of bank notes and hummed as I went up the steps. I wore sandals without socks, and it was fresh and delightful. I wanted to put the money in the bank just as soon as our dear, good banker Fernando had got on his feet.

Up on the Piazza del Sole there were traces of the night before. Streamers and empty bottles, a few pieces of clothing. Mario, good man, was going around with a broom outside the door to his bar; he puckered up his lips and sang:

> "The very nicest thing I know
> Is love, is love…!
> The very loveliest thing I know
> Is lo-o-o-o-ve, ohhh!"

He went in behind the counter, swept a little, bent down and picked up a pink, feminine garment which he laid on the bar.

"*Carissimo*, very best of all waiters! Will you in the goodness of your heart give me a double espresso," I said, "provided that your excellent coffee maker has been turned on and is well warmed up!"

"*Buonissimo professore*! Do you hear the voice of the sun, singing its golden song in the sky! O *professore*, the sun is like a great flaming rooster, waking us all to breakfast and love! Its cock-a-doodle-doo is like gold to the ear!"

"Mario, you're an extraordinary waiter! You are a Torquato Tasso, a Petrarch and a Giacomo Leopardi of a bartender!"

"Best of all *professori*, you left out Gabriele D'Annunzio and Dino Campara! One shouldn't overlook the moderns! Besides, *reverendissimo professore*, you consciously refrained from mentioning The Divine Alighieri, along with Cino da Pistoia, a poet who is not sufficiently noticed, but whom I myself rate the most highly of all our medieval poets."

"Mario!" I said, "imagine having a people like yours to write for!"

"*Carissimo professore*, we Italians are an exceedingly intelligent people. We are *intelligentissimi*, and that is not to our own glory, it is God who has created us thus! Likewise Italy itself is a great success from the Creator's hand. Yes, life is very beautiful…'*nel aer dolce, qui dal sol s'allegra!*'"

In the mild air which rejoices in the sun...! An expression of deep stillness glided over Mario's face, while the aroma of coffee caressed our nostrils. The shadows in the piazza were light blue and quivered in the sunshine, and the mountains rose with supernal clarity above the town. On a couple of the highest peaks lay a thin lacy layer of snow.

Then we heard a yipping, almost barking sound through the silky morning. A cackling, twittering sound. And out onto the piazza came Arnold, followed by Kari, then Marie, and finally Pamela. All following him in single file, like goslings.

"I know where you got that suitcase!" cried Pamela. "You got it from Tomaso! Yes, you did!"

"What about you?" Marie shrieked back. "You think you have the sole right to carry suitcases for Tomaso? I just gave him a helping hand to try to keep him from harming Arnold!"

Pamela barked back, shrilly and sharply:

"Yes, that was some helping hand! I have to laugh! Ha! Ha!"

And she really did laugh, but it was a joyless, in its way sad, laughter.

"Go ahead and laugh!" sneered Marie.

"Yes! I'm laughing!" yelled the furious Pamela. "Ha! Ha! I'm laughing!"

"You just hate me because you can't speak proper English! You gurgle and snort in your disgusting Mississippi dialect!" retorted Marie.

Tears of humiliation and rage came to Pamela's eyes:

"I suppose you think you're better yourself, with your vile British accent! I know why you snuck down to Tomaso!"

"You bloody, blooming bastard!" said Marie in a friendly tone, but with a clear enunciation. "You're ashamed of being from Mississippi, but you never succeed in hiding it, for you pronounce all your stupid sentences through your nose, and at the same time gurgle the words down in your throat!"

Arnold turned around and said:

"Hush, now! Hush! Can't you keep quiet for a little?"

"Shut up!" answered Marie. "You odious libertine! Not a word from you, you who were so busy with Kari's disgusting books all night!"

"Golly!" said Kari, clutching Arnold's arm. "I don't understand why they're so mad at me. I didn't have anything to do with them suitcases!"

"No," Pamela mimicked her savagely, "it's a completely natural thing!"

"Four coffees, Mario!" said Arnold with dignity. For the first time I saw him as a true paterfamilias. Now he was lying in the bed he had made.

"Imagine!" said Pamela to Marie. "Imagine our having this repulsive girlfriend of his in the house! She's being expelled from the country, and she can't even pay her rent!"

"Good morning, *signore!*" said Mario. "Have you slept well?"

Arnold pointed at his caravan-like family.

"Believe me, yes!" he said. And all at once he pulled himself together and raised his hand for silence. He spoke to the ladies as he pointed at his dark glasses, and he did it with power and authority: "Now think of me a little bit too! Do you think it's fun to go around with two such eyes as I have?"

They hushed, for Arnold had been angry. And he was still exasperated, more of a paterfamilas every minute.

"Silence!" he went on. "Shut your mouths!"

This was the new Arnold; politically he was a finished man, and instead he had become master in his own house. Pamela and Marie looked at each other.

"We won't put up with…" began Marie, but Arnold stopped her with a downright patriarchal gesture. He looked calmly at them.

"If you don't shut up right now," said he, "then you can go back to Mississippi and Whitechapel where you came from!"

He looked at me and groaned.

"Yes, Arnold," I said, "that's how it is when you live with a con-glomeration of so many women at once!"

Marie and Pamela sat down next to each other, tight-lipped.

"The problem is discussed way back in the book of Exodus," I went on. "It has always been hard to introduce new wives into a previously established household."

He sat down.

"I'm not living with a conglomeration of anybody!" he said. "Marie and I will get married just as soon as she gets a little nicer. That's all I'm waiting for."

"Let's eat breakfast," said Marie meekly, but with a glower.

"Let's pipe down at any rate!" continued Arnold. "Kari is a girl in need, and it's out of the question for her not to stay with us for awhile! So long as we have room. Meanwhile I think it's too cold to sit here in the shade."

He got up, and we placed a couple of tables together in the sun and carried out the chairs. We had just sat down when Martin arrived with his miniature pinschers. He was wearing the pink pants, and we were glad to have something else to talk about.

"Good morning, Martin!" said Pamela. "Are you alone?"

"Gracious, yes!" replied Martin, "And I'm so unhappy. I haven't seen hide nor hair of my Georgie-Porgie!"

There was complete silence. We all looked at each other.

"Oh, God!" said Marie. "Where do you suppose he can be?"

"So he didn't come home last night?" said Arnold.

"Gosh, has he disappeared?" said Kari.

Arnold stared straight ahead: "I haven't…seen him since yesterday. Early yesterday…!"

"That's just terrible!" said Marie anxiously.

"Oh!" said Martin, "I'm so unhappy for him!"

We fell silent again. Then Mario brought us some *caffè latte* and Danish pastries.

"Have you seen him, Mario?"

"Alas, no, not since yesterday."

"And he didn't come home last night?"

"No," replied Martin, "he's been gone the whole time! Oh God, you must help me find him!"

"We must search for him!" cried Pamela. "If only he hasn't fallen in the sea!"

"Or off one of the cliffs!" added Marie.

"Or down the stairs!" said Kari. "There are such a lot of stairs here!"

"Then somebody would have found him."

"Yes," I said, "then you get found."

"We must call the police," said Arnold.

"Oh, no!" begged Kari. "Not the police!"

"By the way, how are things with the tailor?" said Arnold.

"Ecch, that's nothing!" replied Martin. "If we could just find Georgie-Porgie! Who saw him last?"

I strained to the utmost to remember, and something vaguely rang a bell, but so much had happened yesterday.

"He was unhappy," said Martin.

"Yes," Marie chimed in, "he was really unhappy, poor thing!"

We all looked up, for from one of the little side streets came the sound of yelling and screeching. It was like the singing of drunken men. And out of the narrow Via de Pescatori, from Fishermen's Street, came the skald Svensson and Georg. Arm in arm, shoulder to shoulder. They were supporting each other through the storm of life. Arnold took off his dark glasses to see better.

> Fifteen men on a dead man's chest,
> Yo-ho-ho and a bottle of rum!

The singers approached slowly and in wide pendulum swings over the piazza. They halted, leaning on each other, in front of our table, and Georg's singing stopped. The skald went on singing by himself for a little while. Then he too fell silent.

Georg pointed at Arnold's two black eyes.

"Arnold," he said in a hollow, husky voice, "have you been mixed up in the class struggle? Now again!"

Martin rose and took Georg by the hand.

"Thank God!" he said. "I've been so worried about you!"

Georg looked at him with narrowed eyes and an expression of the greatest mental concentration.

"Where the hell have we met? I've seen you before!"

Then he turned:

"Hey, Mario, very best Ganymede! Bring out the beer! Make it snappy!"

And then to Arnold:

"I have one thing to say to you: Don't ever get mixed up in the class struggle again! Crime doesn't pay! The world is bad, Arnold, and it just gets worse if we interfere! Every time intellectuals get mixed up in politics, everything gets worse."

He stood still for a moment and looked around, then his eye fell on Martin.

"Hey, but that's Martin! And you were going to the tailor's, poor thing!"

Mario brought the beer, and skald Svensson and Georg sat down at the table. Georg went on talking, but the skald was as silent and faraway as the moon.

Arnold said slowly and resolutely:

"Now that's over! I'm done with politics forever! I'm finished with it. But those of us sitting here have a task of a wholly different kind. A task which needs all our forces!"

We looked at him, and Arnold nodded at Kari.

"There sits a sister in need! Our friend Kari is without a residence permit. We have to go to the police for her before it's too late. There has to be somewhere in the world where we can *exist*! If one of us can be expelled, then we're all in jeopardy. We must stand by Kari through thick and thin. She must get a new permit. The little circle which is gathered here must at all costs stick together! If one of us is in danger, then so are all the rest! None of us must leave Bellapalma!"

"Listen!" I said. "It''s just possible that I can do something about this business! I am, if I may say so, rather closely connected to the chief of police."

"You!"

They all stared at me.

"Yes. Since yesterday. I gave them a small helping hand with the revolution. That is, I supported the police chief's proposal during the preceding debate."

"Anso," said Arnold, "you are truly our white-haired boy!"

"Yes," I said, "I am!"

And I stood up.

"I almost think I can promise," I said, "that Kari's residence permit will be in the mail this evening. But now unfortunately I have a meeting. Adieu, dear friends."

As I left I was followed by all their gazes.

Back in the apartment my mail had already come. There was a card which had been posted the day before, a local card with a picture of Bellapalma's little train station on the back. It was from The Girl, with a greeting and the message that she would be back in Bellapalma in two days. Then I heard footsteps padding up the stairs. A barefoot Tomaso stood brown and smiling on the terrace. He had a couple of bruises and a few scratches, but nothing worse. He had a piece of paper in his hand.

"*Carissimo e grandissimo professore!*"

"*Reverendissimo pescatore!*"

He came all the way in.

"It was an extremely glorious day yesterday, *professore!*"

"Yes, *buonissimo* Tomaso! I just hope that you're not feeling too much pain from the fight?"

"O Madonna, he was exceedingly strong, and I feel a very great fear of him. But it was really no more than I deserved, for it was evil and bad of me to use such words to someone who hadn't done me any wrong. I don't understand it, it must have been the very naughty and bad scirocco which made me like that."

He sat down.

"Have you done your homework, best of all fishermen?"

"Yes," he said, "but it is exceedingly difficult! I have worked a very long time at it. But see for yourself, *professore!*"

He handed me the paper and I looked closely at it.

"Yes," I said, "that's right. And now can you tell me what it's called, best of all fishermen?"

"Oh, yes, *professore*. It's called A! A! A!"

"That's right, Tomaso, and now let's take the next! It is: B! B!… as in Bellapalma, as in banana, as in *barca*! That should be easy. But the form is difficult. Look!"

For awhile we stood and practiced on the paper.

"O *professore*!" he said, "this is a very frightful letter, much harder than the first. My head is simply spinning, *professore!* Can't you tell me a little from your homeland by the North Sea instead?"

"No," I said, "first this. How do you pronounce it?"

"B! B!…as in Bellapalma, and in *barca*!"

"Find more words beginning with B, O *reverendissimo pescatore*!"

"B…B…*bella*, B…B…*bionda*! Yes, *professore!* Like in *blonde*!"

"More!"

"B…B…*baffo! Banca! Bacillo!*"

"Excellent, Tomaso, you've got it. Now just practice writing it at home!"

He stuck the paper and pencil in his pocket.

"*Professore?*"

"Yes?"

"Tell a little! Just a little bit, *professore!*"

"Okay," I said, "in my fatherland the sun doesn't go down at night. It's up all night for the whole summer! It's the so-called midnight sun…*il sole di mezzanotte*!"

He sat down and looked at me, faintly skeptical, then he suppressed a smile.

"The sun is up at night, *professore?*"

"Yes, of course!" I said. "Maybe you don't believe it?"

He was finding it more and more difficult to keep a straight face; he even turned away so as not to offend me by showing it.

"What?" I said, "Do you really think I'm lying? Don't you believe I'm telling the truth?"

"*Buonissimo cugino professore! Carissimo* Anso! Of course I believe you're telling the truth!"

"But then why are you smiling at me?"

"*Professore*, of course I believe what you say. I myself have seen it many times!"

"What, Tomaso! Are you claiming that you have seen *il sole di mezzanotte?*"

"*Veramente, professore!* Oh, exceedingly often. It is very common."

"What? It's common?"

"Yes, here in Italy it's highly usual. An extremely well-known phenomenon!"

He paused and looked at me.

"*Professore*, you are a *bambino*, a little tiny *bambino!* You bet I've often seen it!"

"The midnight sun? Here in Italy?"

"Yes, often, *professore!* Really extremely often!"

He paused for a bit and looked at me, smiling faintly and shaking his head over me.

"It's just that," said he, "it's just, *professore*, that here we call it the moon! *La luna!*"

I was speechless.

"Yes,"said Tomaso, "maybe I'm just a little louse of a fisherman, an earthworm who has the government against him and a beginner in reading, but I'm neither *ignorante* nor *stupido*. And I think it's remarkable that your people, who are so skilled at fishing, haven't yet discovered that the big light which is in the sky at night can't be the same as the one which is there in the daytime! It's really extremely easy to see the difference, *professore!*"

I thought about it.

"Tomaso," I said, "the only explanation must be that in my homeland people never go out during the day. For now that I really think about it, the difference between the sun and the moon—as you call it—isn't difficult to observe."

We both looked out through the door. Behind the terrace the ocean gleamed in the sunshine.

"But of course," said Tomaso, "the sun in Italy is much stronger and brighter than in Denmark!"

"Yes, Tomaso, we have to take that into account too. The sun back home in Lapland is rather gray and pallid, sometimes even brown in color."

"Yes, that I can well believe, *professore*! Now tell me a little more about Sweden."

And I told him many things about my native land.

About the Author

Jens Bjørneboe (1920-1976) was a Norwegian poet, playwright, essayist, and novelist who was arguably one of the most important experimental writers of the mid-twentieth century. He was also a visual artist, a Waldorf School teacher, and a renowned social critic. Although little known in the English-speaking world, his work has been translated into a number of European and world languages and is still highly regarded in Scandinavia. His last major work was *The Sharks* (*Haiene*, 1974) and his most critically acclaimed were the three volumes making up the *The History of Bestiality* trilogy; all have been translated into English by Esther Greenleaf Mürer.

About the Translator

Esther Greenleaf Mürer is a poet and translator who resides in Philadelphia. She has previously translated Bjørneboe's novels *The Sharks* (Norvik/Dufour, 1992), *Moment of Freedom* (Norvik/Dufour, 1999), *Powerhouse* (Norvik/Dufour, 2000), and *The Silence* (Norvik/Dufour, 2000) as well as a number of his essays and poems. She was responsible for the "Jens Bjørneboe in English" website, which was the premiere source of information about Jens Bjørneboe written in English and included translations of his poetry, essays, and excerpts of other works

Jens Bjørneboe: Works in English

Plays

Amputation
Edited by Karl August Kvitko
Two versions of the play, translated by Solrun Hoaas +
supplementary essays
Xenos Books, 2003

The Bird Lovers
Translated by Frederick Wasser
Sun & Moon Press, 1994

Semmelweis
Translated by Joe Martin
Sun and Moon Press, 1999

Novels

Ere the Cock Crows
Translated by Esther Greenleaf Mürer
Includes a re-creation of the original play by the translator
Frayed Edge Press, 2021

Winter in Bellapalma
Translated by Esther Greenleaf Mürer
Frayed Edge Press, 2021

Moment of Freedom: The Heiligenberg Manuscript
Translated by Esther Greenleaf Mürer
Norvik Press/Dufour Editions, 1999 (Re-issued 2017)

Powderhouse: Scientific Afterword and Last Protocol
Translated by Esther Greenleaf Mürer
Norvik Press/Dufour Editions, 2000 (Re-issued 2017)

The Silence: An Anti-Novel and Absolutely the Very Last Protocol
Translated by Esther Greenleaf Mürer
Norvik Press/Dufour Editions, 2000 (Re-issued 2017)

The Sharks: The History of a Crew and a Shipwreck
Translated by Esther Greenleaf Mürer
Norvik Press/Dufour Editions, 1992

Without a Stitch
Translated by Walter Barthold
Grove Press, 1969

The Least of These: A Novel [*Jonas*]
Translated by Bernt Jebsen and Douglas K. Stafford
Bobbs-Merrill, 1959

Essays

The Fear of America Within Us & Other Essays on Politics and Society
Translated by Esther Greenleaf Mürer
Xenos Books, 2016

Degrees of Freedom: Anarchist Essays By and About Jens Bjørneboe
Protocol Press, [1996]

About Bjørneboe and His Work

Jens Bjorneboe: Prophet Without Honor
By Janet Garton
Greenwood, 1985

Keeper of the Protocols: The Works of Jens Bjørneboe in the Crosscurrents of Western Literature
By Joe Martin
Peter Lang, 1996

Website

Jens Bjørneboe in English
Includes translations of essays, poems, and excerpts from larger works, and information and essays about Bjørneboe and his work. This site is no longer being maintained; archived copies can be found at:
https://web.archive.org/web/20100105183016/http://emurer. home.att.net/